Raiders of Concho Flats

Raiders of Concho Flats

MATT LAIDLAW

A Black Horse Western

ROBERT HALE · LONDON

ISBN 0 7090 6466 7

Robert Hale Limited
Clerkenwell House
Clerkenwell Green
London EC1R 0HT

Photoset in North Wales by
Derek Doyle & Associates, Mold, Flintshire.
Printed and bound in Great Britain by
WBC Book Manufacturers Limited, Bridgend

To Alistair John Hurst,
Grandson, and number one fan.

ONE

'There must be more to being a ranger than eating oily sardines and chewin' on two hundred miles or more of trail dust,' Rockwell Lane said disgustedly as he buried the remains of their breakfast and used a branch to brush over the ground's surface.

'Yeah – and searching half of New Mexico for a man don't even exist,' Charlie Rivers said, grunting his own long-smouldering complaint as he heaved on his saddle cinch.

'Oh, Jake Arkle was out there all right. Trouble is he had all the villagers so doggone scared they just gave us that infuriating blank look and shrug of the shoulders every time we asked a question.'

'*No comprendez,*' Rivers echoed bitterly. 'Maybe we should've just stood in the square in Tularosa and hollered his name, waited for him to come crawlin' out of one of them adobes.'

'Wouldn't have done much good. By then I reckon he was already long gone, heading south through the San Andres, making for Las Cruces.'

Or some other godforsaken hell hole, Rockwell

Lane thought, admitting to himself that in truth he had no idea which direction the killer had taken.

Alerted by telegraph from Austin, the two rangers had handed over a double eagle – which she tested with gleaming white teeth – to buy the information from a black-eyed Mexican wench in a Santa Fe bar that Jake Arkle had headed west. He was, she told them, riding a sorrel with a marked left hind shoe. They knew this already, and so considered the money well spent. Acting on her information they picked up Arkle's trail as they cut across country to the Bravo, and with the conviction that they were closing they followed the outlaw's thin sign clear down to Albuquerque.

But somewhere between there and the Malpais they'd lost him. The ride to Tularosa had been wasted effort. As Rockwell Lane had pointed out as both rangers gazed over a blistering landscape of saw-toothed sierra and waterless, dust-caked foothills, Jake Arkle could have headed west through the Jornada del Muerto with his mind set on making the long run for the Gila and Arizona, or ridden south down the San Andres towards El Paso del Norte.

At sunset on the fourteenth day they'd given up the chase. Next morning they'd swung about to head for Texas. On weary horses they negotiated the jagged ridges and tortuous ravines of the Guadalupe Mountains, and got a brief taste of searing heat as they skirted the southern bluffs of the Llano Estacado. It was with immense relief that they came down from the dazzling white escarpments and rode south east down Mustang Draw towards the Concho.

But it was a relief that for Ranger Rockwell Lane was spoiled somewhat by the knowledge that when they reached Austin, he'd have some explaining to do. They were Texas Rangers, and they'd lost Jake Arkle.

'San Andres, Las Cruces,' Rivers said now, without conviction. 'Seems to me like this whole darn business has been full of "maybes" and "ifs".'

'So here's a couple more,' Rockwell Lane said, his tone suddenly holding a new, sharp note of warning. '*Maybe* you'd better get over here with your saddle gun, Charlie, *if* you don't want to get caught with your pants down. We're about to have company – and that's a certainty.'

Instantly, in a sequence of swift, practised movements, Rivers slid his Spencer out of its scabbard, ran towards the ridge, then hit the dew-soaked grass and snaked up behind a clump of beaded mesquite that afforded some cover but allowed him a clear view.

Lane was already flat on his belly, his black Stetson tipped forwards to shield his eyes as he gazed into the near distance.

They had made camp the previous day on a low knoll, where a hollow of lush grass watered by a shallow pool provided feed for their horses, and a grove of trees afforded relief from the blazing summer sun. It also gave them a clear view for many miles in every direction, so Rockwell Lane was able to give an accurate assessment of the tragedy that was about to happen.

'Whoever he is, that feller's got no place left to go,' he said, and spat disgustedly into the parched mesquite. 'And if he could find a hole to crawl into, that wrung-out horse he's on'd die before it got him there.'

The early morning sun was a red disc painted on the orange-streaked eastern skyline, and was not yet warm. Mist that lay like a thin white blanket over the land between the north and middle Conchos transformed the limitless plains into a landscape that deceived the eyes. But the single rider in the white shirt desperately flogging his jaded horse towards the gleaming waters of the big bend in the middle Concho was no illusion, and the three horsemen riding in a ragged, extended line half a mile back – no more than ugly black shapes riding out of the sun – were swiftly closing on their quarry.

'Heading for San Angelo. Sure must have a reason for ridin' that horse so hard,' Rivers observed. 'Posse chasing him – or bandits after something that feller's carrying?'

'We've got maybe a couple of minutes to decide,' Lane said, 'and not a lot to tell us which way to jump.' He rolled away from the ridge, climbed to his feet and moved quickly to the stand of pines where their horses were tethered.

He was a tall man, Rockwell Lane, with a rawboned strength in his long limbs and a laziness in his movements as he reached for his pouched Winchester, that had led lesser men to believe him easy meat. But those men had neglected to look into the deep-set eyes spaced wide over high cheek-bones and a sensitive mouth. If they had done so they would have seen shining there the implacable will of a man for whom defeat was an unknown word. For many of them, that would have been the last picture they took with them to Hades. That, and the thin smile – it might have been one of sadness – that always flickered across Lane's angular countenance at such moments.

'Me, I'd side with the underdog every time,' Charlie Rivers offered as Lane jacked a shell into the Winchester's breech and came back through the damp grass.

As tow-headed as his partner was dark, and of no more than average height, Rivers was stretched out with his old Spencer pointing casually towards the approaching riders. Even in repose his hard, sinewy build was impressive, the unusually wide shoulders seemingly built to take the kick of the powerful rifle. Whereas Rockwell Lane's face was slow to break into a smile, his brown eyes always thoughtful, Rivers usually had a twinkle in his sharp blue eyes and a smile lurking around the corners of his wide mouth.

But now, as he eased the butt of the Spencer into his shoulder, he was scowling, and there was a note of righteous anger in his voice.

'So, which is it to be, Rocky?'

'Well, if we side with the feller being chased,'

Rockwell Lane said, 'we're outgunned three to two.'

'Hell, last time we had such favourable odds was when we caught them three Sioux slicing beef steaks off a maverick steer,' Rivers said. He flashed his partner a tight grin, then flattened his cheek against the Spencer and squeezed the trigger.

The crack of the shot sent birds soaring and wheeling from the tall trees. It was as if the chill, misted air rippled as the bullet sped towards the racing horsemen. Rockwell Lane settled down some yards away and snugged the Winchester into his shoulder. As he did so a faint cry drifted to his ears, and a rider out on the flank pointed towards the knoll and swerved his horse violently.

'Reckon they know we're here,' Lane said. He took careful aim and the Winchester bucked as he sent a bullet screaming uncomfortably low over the head of the centre rider. Distinguishable now as a big, bulky man, he flattened himself along his horse's straining neck, but kept coming hard and fast. And now all three riders were eating up the ground between them and the lone figure spurring the weary bronc.

'Seems wrong to blast 'em out of the saddle,' Lane said pensively, 'when we don't know what the hell's goin' on.' Posse or renegades, he thought, squinting at the fast-moving drama being enacted under the lightening skies. Innocent man – or a killer about to get his just deserts?

'If we don't do something, that feller dies,' Rivers said, but his voice, too, was uncertain.

'Maybe if he makes the river...' Lane began, then smiled fleetingly as he realized that once again he was putting voice to conjecture.

Then the crackle of pistol fire interrupted their musings. Puffs of smoke erupted from six-guns as the chasing men, judging they were in pistol range, sent a hail of lead screaming towards the desperate rider.

For a few, fleeting moments it seemed as if he would emerge from the volley unscathed. Then, as Rockwell Lane watched with eyes grown suddenly bleak, the fugitive jerked back his head and arched his back. For an instant he tried to hang there, tossing bonelessly on the horse's back, white face lifted to the skies. Then he toppled from the saddle. One boot caught in a stirrup and he was dragged, bouncing. Like a sack of grain the slack body towed a trail of dust almost to the river's edge before the snagged foot slipped free. As the horse trotted away into the shallows the man rolled, then flopped limply over the river bank and lay still. Both legs were half-submerged to the waist in the gently lapping water. His arms were flung wide, his face buried in the sand.

'I guess that settles it,' Lane said grimly.

The three gunmen were much closer to the river now, converging as they thundered down on their victim. Pistols glittered in their gloved hands. Even at a distance of 150 yards, Lane could distinguish dark, unshaven faces bearing expressions of savage intent.

Once again Rockwell Lane lined up the Winchester on the middle rider, a burly figure in dusty black garb. But this time he offered him no warning. He squinted along the sights, centred on the man's broad chest and blasted a shot.

The heavy figure was slammed backwards out of the saddle. As the gunman tumbled helplessly over his horse's flying tail, Charlie Rivers's Spencer roared and another man yelled in pain and anger.

Then the two remaining riders, mounted on a fast, rangy buckskin and a big bay, reached the river. They rode recklessly over the low, vertical bank and raced through the shallows, flying spray sparkling like droplets of blood against the morning sunlight. Cursing through clenched teeth, Rockwell Lane and Charlie Rivers fired again. Both shots went low and wide, kicking up sand. But now killers and victim were too close together for further shots to be risked.

The two rangers watched with grim faces and narrowed eyes as the two riders reached the body lying half in the water. They rode past on either side, cutting in close. The man on the buckskin cut it too fine; a pounding hoof raised dust as it thudded into the prone man's shoulder.

And then, in the fraction of a second they were alongside, each rider leaned out of the saddle and cold-bloodedly shot the man in the back.

A laugh rang out, clear on the morning air, and the man on the bay lifted his hand in triumph.

'Murdering bastards!'

The expletive was torn from Lane's lips as again

he triggered a shot. But now the men were swinging their horses wide, once more riding a diverging course as they urged their mounts across the sun-painted waters.

It seemed as if they were heading straight for the knoll. A fierce fusillade of pistol shots sent bullets hammering into the ridge, showering the rangers with dirt. They dropped flat, hugging the grass. But when the firing abruptly ceased and they cautiously lifted their heads, the two gunmen were more than fifty yards upstream.

They spurred their horses up onto the bank, streaming water. As they sped away, another shot from Charlie Rivers plucked a black hat and tossed it high as he swung the big Spencer to follow the racing horses. A third clipped the big bay's flank, and its thin squeal trailed behind it as it raced away from the river.

Out on the open plain the killers rode with distance between them, skilfully directing their horses into a fast, swerving gallop. Twin plumes of dust rose in thin clouds, mingling with the hanging mist to make accurate rifle fire impossible. Rivers's Spencer cracked as he swore through clenched teeth. The thunder of racing hooves began to fade. Sunlight winked on metal, caught the flash of skin as one rider glanced back. Then they were over a low rise and as they raced down the far slope they came together and swung north-west so that a thick stand of trees that poked through the mist was between them and the two rangers.

'Leave 'em,' Lane gritted.

'San Angelo's due east,' Charlie Rivers said, grounding his rifle as he squinted calculatingly into the drifting dust. 'They ain't headed that way.'

'We'll come to that. First, let's see if anyone's alive.'

Rockwell Lane was first off the knoll, flinging himself into the saddle then ramming the Winchester into the boot under his left thigh as he sent his powerful dun gelding streaking down the shallow slope and made for the river.

At the big, sweeping ox-bow the middle Concho was wide, but shallow. Lane took his horse across fast, its flashing hooves beating the icy water to a white foam. As he approached the far bank his heart sank within him. The lone rider's white shirt was soaked with bright red blood. He had not lifted his face from the sand.

Lane leaped from the saddle without drawing rein, and as the dun trotted away he dropped to his knees alongside the still, bloody figure. Conscious of Charlie Rivers splashing towards him, he took hold of the man's shoulder and gently rolled him over onto his back.

Shock was like a solid punch, rocking him back on his heels.

Behind him, Charlie Rivers's boots crunched in the wet sand. 'Judas Priest!' he said in hushed tones. 'They murdered a woman!'

'A girl,' Lane said tightly.

Instinctively he reached down to brush coarse,

wet sand from a hauntingly beautiful face that would never feel his touch. The eyes were closed, dark lashes lying on pale cheeks. She had been no more than eighteen, Lane reckoned – and she had been hunted down like a rabid dog, her young body riddled with bullets fired by men who knew they were being watched.

'Must be pretty damn sure of themselves,' he mused.

'Or operate so far outside the law they no longer abide by any rules,' Charlie Rivers said. He moved away from the girl's body to look over the low bank and said, 'The feller you shot is wearing old Union pants and shirt. Renegades was right. What we've got here is part of a bunch of jayhawkers, Rocky – though why they went to all that trouble to ride down and kill a young girl has got me beat.'

'San Angelo's maybe ten miles east,' Rockwell Lane said, climbing up off his knees. 'About the same distance west of the river's that cluster of shacks we skirted before we bedded down.'

He brushed off wet sand and stretched to his full height, whistled softly to call the gelding, caught his partner's nod of understanding.

'Town called Concho Flats,' Rivers said, his face grim at the recollection. 'They didn't come from there, but that's surely the miserable hole they're headed for.'

'There's a scattering of ranches in these parts,' Lane went on. 'One I know of is up on the North Concho, a pretty powerful outfit run by a fiery old

Virginian, name of Sam Wallace, who came out west for his health and made himself a fortune. Or,' he said, gathering the trailing reins as the gelding reached him, 'it was powerful when the War started. What it's like after four years of slaughter is any man's guess.'

'And you're saying these men are part of that outfit? Maybe the girl, too?' Charlie Rivers questioned, frowning.

'I don't know what I'm saying,' Lane admitted. 'Thinking out loud is the best way I can put it, Charlie – but what I do know is I'm takin' these bodies into that town called Concho Flats, and then I'm going to do some digging.'

'Uh huh.' For the first time since witnessing the sickening killing of the young girl, Charlie Rivers flashed a knowing grin. 'That should occupy us for days, maybe even weeks – and what you're hoping is when we do eventually ride into Austin, tempers will have cooled, the small matter of Jake Arkle become somewhat faded—'

'Mount up,' Lane snapped.

'Yes, sir!' Rivers returned, grinning broadly now.

By the time they had rounded up the loose horses and lashed the bodies belly-down over the saddles – the girl's tenderly, the big man in the faded Union garb roughly and with several muttered curses – the sun was well up, the river mist thinning in its heat.

Dashing sweat from his brow with his sleeve, Lane planted his stiff-brimmed black hat on his head and said, 'You winged one of those killers, Charlie.

There's also a big bay horse carrying a bloody gash. That should make 'em easy enough to find.'

He finished tying the lead ropes, stepped up into the saddle and looked thoughtfully across at Rivers, sitting comfortably atop his horse with his hands folded on the horn.

'If two of us ride into Concho Flats, all our cards are on the table, face up,' Lane said, again doing his thinking the way he often did – out loud. 'Might make a better start at getting to the bottom of this if you head north. Ride a wide sweep, come into that big spread from the far side, act like you're a drifter looking for work.'

Rivers pursed his lips. 'And if the War's taken its toll – and that feller lyin' belly down is anything to go by – could be a different kind of work from that you've got in mind.'

'No.' Lane allowed himself a thin smile. 'I've got a pretty good idea of what's likely to be on offer, but you always were better with a gun than a rope. . . .'

Saddle leather creaked as Rockwell Lane eased the big gelding forward and took up slack in the trail ropes. He turned as he moved the three horses towards the pines and the far side of the knoll, then yelled, 'Just so's you know where you're going, if I recall the name right, you'll be ridin' into the Running Irons.' He saw Rivers's wave of acknowledgement, and watched the slim ranger splash through the shallow waters of the Concho.

Then, with a final grim look back at the cargo he was carrying, Rockwell Lane turned towards the decaying settlement on which someone with a twisted sense of humour or a mountain of optimism had bestowed the pleasant name of Concho Flats.

TWO

From some distance out the outlines of the town appeared through the forming heat haze like a wide-spaced cluster of crude timber crates that, countless years ago, had fallen heavily from an ox train and been left on the plains by the weary wagonmaster to bleach in the sun.

Far beyond to the south-west, almost lost in the shimmer, the ruined adobe buildings of the Mission San Luis were like buff-coloured rocks poking up out of the limitless grass.

As Rockwell Lane led the two horses at a walk past the outlying shacks he saw that Concho Flats boasted no main street but instead had at its centre an open space – eighty or ninety yards across – which, in one of the grander towns across the border, might have served as a plaza.

But in place of the sturdy, white adobe dwellings and stores that would have lent a picturesque charm and grace to such a square, false-fronted business establishments that had never seen a lick of paint leaned drunkenly in haphazard groups around this uneven area dotted with patches of parched grass and criss-crossed by old wagon ruts. Here and there a rickety plankwalk was shaded by an overhang supported by uprights bearing scars inflicted by bullet and knife. Alleyways between those structures that adjoined one another were choked with refuse.

As far as Lane could see, the only stone building in the town was the Concho Flats bank, which stood alongside a single-storey timber café with a sagging shingle roof. His failure to find the barred windows of a jail only confirmed what he had expected: if a citizen of Concho Flats wanted the assistance of the law, he would need to ride to San Angelo.

Eddies of drifting dust caused Lane to squint as he rode into the heart of Concho Flats, for with the sun a light wind had arisen that swirled erratically around and between the buildings. A tumbleweed skittered across his path and was bowled on before the breeze until finally coming to rest against the side wall of the town's livery stable behind which a big corral stood empty. An unseen dog howled, sending a shiver down Lane's spine, and through narrowed eyes he looked beyond the stable to a general store.

As he bore down on it, two men heaving a sack of grain onto a buckboard glanced up, and were about to return to their lifting when their eyes were caught by the following horses and their gruesome loads. Shock hit them as they saw the girl's dark hair, the blood-soaked shirt. The sack of grain fell, and burst open. Ignoring it, both men leaped up onto the gallery and ran into the store, and as Lane passed by he saw the flash of a white apron in the shadowy interior. He was aware, without looking back, that the man wearing that apron had emerged to watch his progress.

Rockwell Lane stowed that knowledge for future reference, tacked onto it the reminder that in small towns the general store would stock new weapons, and their ammunition – then deliberately put those thoughts to the back of his mind.

Then he was drawing close to another two-storey building, set back from the dust bowl that was Concho Flats's square. Its first-floor windows were blinded by filthy muslin curtains. Below them, set back under the overhang, batwing doors opened off a canted plankwalk. The flaking sign nailed above this gallery told Rockwell Lane he was approaching Reilly's Pleasure Palace.

As he dismounted and tied up, Lane noted that two of the half dozen horses at the hitch rail, a rangy buckskin and a big bay, were lathered, the white sweat now dried to a hard crust by the hot sun. On one of them, the bay, that dried sweat was streaked with blood. The other wrung-out horse, the buckskin, was rigged with a McClellan saddle whose left fender was also streaked with blood.

And it was only after long moments of staring thoughtfully at those clear messages of guilt that he had known all along he would find here that Rockwell Lane became aware of the creaking of the batwings' hinges, the measured tread of boots on loose timber.

'Hell, you've got some gall!'

The man was tall and lean, his voice breathless. A sweat-stained black hat shaded a face that was unshaven and scarred and inherently vicious. A liberal film of trail dust coated the man's hat, his filthy woollen shirt, the faded blue trousers with the yellow stripe down the outside of each leg. Twin Colts in greased leather holsters encircled the man's hips, and even the jolt glass of whiskey held loosely in his right hand – that might, conceivably, Lane thought, slow his reactions – did nothing to detract from their menace.

'Since when does bringing dead folk into town for a decent burial require nerve?'

Lane stepped up onto the plankwalk, and with a swift glance into the tall man's colourless eyes he brushed past and went on into the thick gloom that reeked of stale beer and cigarette smoke, and was as silent as the grave. A red-haired, red-faced, blue-eyed barman about the size of an average buffalo watched his approach, big hands flat on the heavy oak bar. Behind the bar a fly-blown mirror threw Lane's reflection in his face as he picked his way through the empty tables, a dark silhouette outlined against the bright rectangle of the door.

A second shape filled that brightness as the tall gunman followed him inside and stood blocking the exit.

'You Reilly?' Lane enquired of the barman.

'Mick Reilly, or my mother was a liar, but as she died before I was born and I never knew my father. . . .' The blue eyes twinkled. 'What was the question again?'

Feeling the muscles in his back begin to crawl, Lane said amiably, 'What justifies that sign over the door, Mick?'

The big man cast a glance over at the battered piano and the dusty faro tables, then winked broadly. 'I suppose it all depends on your notion of pleasure – or maybe it's just that you've walked in at the wrong time of day.'

'Maybe I have at that,' Lane agreed. 'A beer, Mick, cold if you've got it, otherwise as it comes.'

'As it comes is what you get,' Reilly said, pouring beer from a jug while maintaining a straight face, 'because the only certain cold place in Concho Flats is the widow Logan's bed. Although,' he added, 'I'd rather you didn't tell a certain Lije Coombs I said that.'

Lane used his left hand to accept the glass, washed the dust from his throat with a copious draught of the lukewarm liquid, then turned to face the room as a man coughed drily.

Sprawled in a chair behind a table close to the window, a slender man with a sweeping black moustache was watching him with amused, liquid dark eyes of the kind that are apt to switch instantly from good humour to controlled fury, from a spurious friendliness to intense hatred. Lane figured him to be part bad Mexican, part renegade Indian, with maybe some mean white tossed in to dilute the mix without reducing the strength. The man was hatless – hell, he would be, Lane thought: his hat's ten miles back, punctured by one of Charlie Rivers's bullets. A silk vest decorated with silver conchos was open to expose a faded black shirt. Tight Mexican pants were tucked into expensive, tooled leather boots.

His left leg was propped up on another chair, the black pants torn and stiff with blood. One of the man's slim hands rested on the table. A cocked six-gun held in it pointed lazily at Rockwell Lane's belt buckle.

The tall gunman who had followed Lane into the saloon remained by the door. His shadow lay long across the sawdust.

'What Zac Slaughter really means when he talks about nerve,' the man at the table explained casually, 'is foolishness. Because only a fool'd ride into Concho Flats with two bodies, one of them Jake Arkle's top gun, the other the only daughter of the biggest rancher on the Concho.'

'Did I miss some signal?' Lane asked, his mind freezing at the mention of Arkle's name, 'or can you see clear through walls? I made no mention of any woman.'

'You denyin' it, friend?'

'Just askin' how you know.'

'Settin' that to one side for a while, why don't you tell us how you expect to get away with this. You can't walk out of here with my pistol pointin' at your belly – and don't tell us you've got friends waitin' outside, because you ain't.'

Lane drained the glass, set it down on the bar.

'No,' he said. 'I rode in alone. I'm a drifter, spent the night bedded down on a knoll alongside the middle Concho, woke up in time to watch three men gun down that girl.'

'So if they was gunnin' down an unarmed girl, what did Hackett do – shoot himself by accident?'

Lane shrugged, and looked pointedly at the man's injured leg. 'If he did, that makes two of you before the sun was all the way up.'

The man at the door chuckled breathlessly and stepped further into the room. The empty shot glass formed a glittering arc cutting through the shaft of sunlight as he tossed it to the bartender.

'Why don't we just string him up, Quatro,' he said, 'before he chokes himself to death on all them accusations and lies?'

'Maybe you'd better check with Jake Arkle before you join in all that foolishness you mentioned,' Rockwell Lane said casually. He looked directly at the seated man as he spoke, saw renewed interest in the dark eyes. With his back resting easily against the bar he took a sack of Bull Durham from his shirt pocket and began to roll a smoke while listening with some amusement to the sudden silence.

He knew full well that there was no way Arkle could have ridden from wherever the hell he'd vanished to inside Mexico and beaten the two rangers to the Concho. But if the dead man was

Arkle's top gun, then somehow Jake Arkle had a hand in whatever was going on around Concho Flats, and these two men would be wary of moving without his say-so. Both of them had been in on the killing at the Concho, and it was Lane's guess that they were aware that two men had opened fire on them from the knoll. They were suspicious, thought he might be one of them but couldn't be sure. If he was, they wanted to know the whereabouts of the second man – and killing Lane wouldn't give them the answer.

Abruptly, the man called Quatro kicked his injured leg off the chair, climbed stiffly to his feet and pouched his six-gun.

'Zac, you get over to the store, let Olsen and Patchet know what's happened. Get them to load Jean Wallace's body onto the buckboard and take her out to the Running Irons. If we ride fast, we'll overtake them on the trail. Arkle needs to know what's happened before the buckboard gets there. Sam Wallace'll blow his top – which ain't no problem – but when he cools down he might start thinking all the wrong thoughts.'

As Slaughter nodded and left the saloon, Quatro fixed Lane with a glance that was both angry and puzzled.

'So what the hell do you know about Jake Arkle?'

'Only that, wherever he is, he ain't out at the Running Irons.'

'How come you're so sure of that?'

'I already told you I'm a drifter. A man passing

through makes a point of keeping his eyes and ears open. Last I heard of Jake Arkle, he was heading down the Bravo towards Juarez.'

Again Quatro's black eyes looked speculatively at Rockwell Lane, taking in the tall man's lean, muscular frame, the steady eyes with their cool, fearless gaze, the relaxed hands going about their work with paper and tobacco; the single Colt in the tied-down holster.

'You always drift?' he said softly. 'Or, at the right time, and in the right place—'

'And for the right money?' Lane suggested, and cocked an eyebrow as he applied a match to the cigarette and looked at Quatro through the flame.

'Yeah,' Quatro said, and now the dark gaze was knowing, the thin lips twisting into a satisfied smirk. 'I had you figured, feller. If the money's right, that gun's for hire – ain't that right?'

Tongue in cheek, but with complete honesty, Rockwell Lane said, 'It's been for hire for the past ten years. A man has to make his living the best way he knows how—'

'Don't he just!' Quatro turned away and limped towards the door. As Lane followed and they stepped out onto the sun-drenched plankwalk and looked across towards the store he said, 'My advice to you is get the hell out of Concho Flats. All right, you look like a feller can handle himself when the shooting starts. But the man bossing the show out at the Running Irons ain't going to be too damn happy about what happened to Hackett—'

'I told you,' Lane said carefully, 'I saw what happened, but had no hand in the girl's death.'

'And I'm telling you,' Quatro said, laughing, 'forget the girl, start worryin' about your own skin.'

Zac Slaughter had unhitched the dead girl's horse and led it across the square. The two men who had hard-eyed Lane as he entered Concho Flats were lifting the limp form and laying it between the sacks of grain. Voices drifted on the hot air, and to Lane it seemed that Slaughter was arguing a point with the man in the white apron who had charged out of the store like an angry bull. Then, as the two men climbed aboard the buckboard and set it rolling away towards the edge of town, Slaughter jerked on the reins and swung his mount angrily around in a tight circle to send a swift glance over towards the saloon.

'This feller you mentioned out at the Running Irons,' Lane said innocently, as Quatro acknowledged Slaughter's impatient wave and stepped around to mount his horse on the Indian side in order to kick his stiff left leg over the saddle. 'Would that be Jake Arkle?'

'Didn't you just tell me?' Quatro called over his shoulder as he wheeled the big bay and headed across the square towards the store. 'Jake's heading down the Bravo to Juarez.'

'Yeah,' Rockwell Lane said softly, as the two men rode after the buckboard at a fast gallop. 'That's what I thought – but now, well, I guess someone's lyin' through their back teeth, or me and Charlie have wasted time chasing a mirage.'

The squeak of wheels and the sound of a horse blowing issued from a shaded alley alongside the livery stable, and Lane stared in astonishment as a magnificent black hearse of glass and timber burst forth into the sunlit square and a bone-thin man wearing a battered top hat and long frock-coat brought it rattling across the square towards the dozing horse bearing the body of the man called Hackett.

Well, it looks like there's one line of business that's highly profitable in these parts, Lane thought, and as the hearse made a wide sweep to come in alongside the hitch rail outside Reilly's Pleasure Palace he raked the almost empty square with one final glance then stepped down from the plankwalk, unhitched his dun and led it at an angle towards the livery stable.

From the gallery outside the store, the man in the apron watched him all the way. Then he went back into the store, to emerge a few moments later with a shotgun cradled in his left arm. He walked to the end of the plankwalk, jumped down into the dust, and with the twin barrels gleaming in the sun he headed towards the stable.

The gloom inside the stable left Lane momentarily blinded. Then, as his eyes adjusted, he saw a wide runway lined with stalls sloping gently down to a back entrance that opened onto the wide, empty corral flanked by outlying sheds for shoeing, storing meadow-hay, or lining up buggies and wagons.

Expecting a stale smell of caked horse ordure and sour straw, he was pleasantly surprised to detect only sweetness and the pleasing odours of leather, saddle soap and fresh oats. And when the ostler emerged, grumbling good-naturedly, from the rickety office nailed together just inside the wide front entrance, Lane saw untidy brown hair and eyes like hazy morning skies gazing keenly at him from a nest of fine wrinkles, in a face with the skin of a dried out apple. Short and wiry, wearing a faded denim shirt and brown cord pants, the ostler was twenty going on forty, and, although he looked like a man who would be at home atop a racehorse, he wore a six-gun in a tied-down holster more appropriate for a border gunslinger. Those eyes shifted from Lane to the dun gelding, and in them there was a subtle change and Lane grinned as he recognized the signs.

'You must be the most contented man I've seen since I rode into Concho Flats,' he said, and was rewarded by a terse answer that succinctly explained the philosophy that shone brightly in those eyes.

'Deal with horses, not men,' the ostler said, in a voice like loose gravel. 'Got two back there with the blood of Arabs and the temperament of a saint, ain't met one yet that was as ornery as most two-legged varmints.'

'Oh, I don't know,' Lane said, grinning as he handed the man the reins. 'Climbed atop an old outlaw bronc one time, he swapped ends so fast he damn near screwed himself and me into the ground – but I must admit, he was an exception.'

'Yeah, and that tale's got more whiskers on it than my chin, and is just about as tall as the feller just walked in through the door,' the ostler scoffed.

Lane turned to gaze up at the man in the frock-coat and battered top hat. This close up he was as thin and parched as a dried-out sapling. In his shiny stovepipe boots he stood some six and a half feet tall, the high crowned hat pushing that closer to seven.

'Mister,' he said, looking mournfully at Lane, 'that feller you brung in belly down's inside my hearse. We have a fine cemetery here in Concho Flats and at this time of the year it don't take long for the hot sun to make dead folks a mite obnoxious to the nose – so if you've got any objections or special instructions I'd like to hear them before I make haste to plant him six feet under.'

Lane shook his head. 'Talk to some of his friends, I—'

'That's exactly what he is doing,' a harsh voice cut in.

And as Rockwell Lane swung to face the speaker he was met by the deadly sound of oiled twin hammers cocking. For the second time in the space of an hour he found himself staring into the black muzzle of a gun lined up on his belt buckle.

THREE

The route Charlie Rivers set out to follow to the Running Irons was a straight line west followed by a wide, sweeping loop that would eventually see him pointing his horse's nose back in the direction of the Middle Concho. So for some distance it ran parallel to the one taken by Rockwell Lane on his way to Concho Flats, though on the opposite bank of the river.

For several miles Rivers was able to watch the progress of his partner and the two led horses with their grisly burdens, though he guessed rightly that Lane was too intent with his own thoughts and on watching his front to let his gaze wander.

Eventually, when the roofs of the town appeared like a cluster of crumbling anthills through the haze – by which time Lane and his horses, on a gradually diverging course, had been reduced by distance to the size of crawling ants – Rivers forsook his own westerly route and began the circle that would see him covering twenty miles to reach a destination that in a straight line was no more than ten miles away. Tiresome, but by no means a waste of time; it would bring him in behind the buildings of the distant ranch as if he'd ridden directly south from the Cap Rock across the Colorado and North Concho, thus reducing the likelihood of his being linked to Rockwell Lane.

It also gave him plenty of time to figure out what he was going to do and say when he reached the Running Irons.

The ride was mostly over rich, undulating grass-land criss-crossed by wide, rutted cattle trails, with here and there clusters of pecans or live-oak thick-ets that would afford some shade if he chose to stop. He did that once only. After ten of those twenty miles he rode into a sparse grove of willows that had sprung up alongside a gurgling stream that was a run-off from the big river, and there took time to fashion a cigarette while sitting with his back up against the bole of a tree.

With the cigarette fired up, he watched with some pleasure as his fine blue roan cropped the lush grass and enjoyed the luxury of a slackened cinch.

So, Ranger Charlie Rivers mused, what the hell were three Yankee jayhawkers doing ridin' out at dawn to murder a young girl?

The answer was far from clear and, as he trickled smoke, tipped his hat forward and half closed his eyes, Rivers found himself mentally traversing the miles in an attempt to pick the brains of a partner he had ridden stirrup with for more than ten years, and whose opinion and views on life in general –

and rangering in particular – he valued more than those of any other man on earth.

'But right now I guess he's got no more idea of what's goin' on than I have,' he told his grazing horse, 'which leaves me ridin' blind into a situation that could be just a mite uncomfortable, or about ready to explode.'

Anytime Captain Rockwell Lane was mystified or perplexed or just plain undecided – all of which were rare occurrences – Charlie Rivers began to feel uneasy. He felt the first itchings of that discomfiture now. Nevertheless, he conceded that Rocky was handling the situation sensibly, with due respect for the risks involved.

The fact that they were hundreds of miles away from the hot, wearisome pursuit of the outlaw Jake Arkle was one big worry off both their minds, though undoubtedly a source of future irritation for the authorities back in Austin. And with that thought bringing the ever-ready grin back to crease his face, Rivers climbed to his feet, flicked the cigarette into the gently tinkling stream, then settled his hat firmly on his unruly fair hair and whistled to his horse.

When he'd tightened the cinch and stepped up into the saddle he was interested to see, in the far distance, a plume of dust being kicked up by a wagon and two horses heading due east at a fast lick.

'Well, now,' Rivers murmured, and he folded his hands on the horn and did some deep pondering.

The only place near enough for that wagon to

have come from was Concho Flats. The first place it would hit in the direction it was headed was the Running Irons.

For one crazy moment as he sat astride the roan the sight of two horses so soon after he'd left the Concho had Rivers convinced that Rockwell Lane had for some reason changed his plan and was riding to meet him at the ranch.

Then common sense took over.

Even from a distance he could see the two horses had riders. Most likely they were ranch hands. They'd accompanied the wagon into town the previous day, spent the night on the town and were heading back to the ranch with provisions. But if that was all there was to it – why the hurry?

Because, Rivers decided, the two rangers had inadvertently poked a long stick into a distant hornets' nest.

Rockwell Lane had taken two bodies into town. One of those bodies had been that of a girl. Lane had surmised that, for some reason connected with Yankee renegades, she had been fleeing towards the Concho from the Running Irons with the intention of reaching San Angelo.

The other body had been that of a dead jayhawker.

The rangers had also surmised that the two jayhawkers left alive after the killing had been making for Concho Flats. If they were right, then once Lane rode into town, the sight of either one of the two bodies by opposing factions would have inflamed passions and been likely to cause all hell to break loose.

But, Rivers ruminated, where did all that leave him?

Once again, as was his custom when alone and forced to reach a decision, he enlisted the help of the thoughts and wisdom of his friend, mentor and superior officer, Captain Rockwell Lane.

What Rocky would do in the changed circumstances, he decided, would be to go ahead more or less as planned, but with a slight change of timing. Everything that had transpired that morning seemed to point towards the Running Irons. Instead of continuing on his circular route, his best bet now was to head straight towards the ranch. That way he'd reach it not too long after the wagon and riders. In time, he hoped, to find out what the hell was setting their pants on fire, and maybe save his own from getting fatally singed.

The decision reached, Charlie Rivers left the grove of willows at a canter, touched the roan lightly with his heels and lifted it to a stretched-out gallop. The warm breeze of his passing flattened the brim of his hat. The plume of dust he watched with narrowed blue eyes was an arrow tail slanting its way across the grass, the wagon and riders the dark arrow-head.

In his mind's eye Charlie Rivers could see the point where the arrow head would cut across his own trail. After fifteen minutes' hard riding, the imagined point became reality: the buildings of the Running Irons ranch hove into sight nestled snugly between low hills topped with pines, and Rivers knew that he was going to arrive there too late.

'Easy, boy,' he murmured, and he patted the roan's damp neck and sat upright as the pace slackened. And in that manner, relaxed in body but with a mind filled with conjecture – full of those ifs and maybes, he thought, remembering with warm amusement the conversation at the Concho – Charlie Rivers rode down a long, grassy slope to arrive at the big ranch some five minutes after the wagon and riders.

He rode into a big yard flanked by a sprawling ranch house with a wide gallery along its front, two high barns, a long, low, log bunkhouse whose door gaped wide. Two peeled-pole corrals were visible behind the barns. In one, horses circled nervously, their ears pricked. The other was empty. The smell of fried bacon was carried on air still powdery with the wagon's dust.

The wagon was at a standstill close to the hitch rail in front of the house. The front door was open, and as Rivers drew near an imposing, rawboned man with a shock of iron-grey hair emerged onto the wide gallery and stepped down into the dust. He could have been any age between forty and sixty, and Rivers opted for midway. Behind him as he strode bareheaded in the sunlight there walked a younger man, no more than twenty years old, dark of countenance but bearing an uncanny resemblance to the older man, following with less haste.

Sam Wallace and his son, Rivers guessed, and

even from a distance he could see the bright blood staining the older man's hands.

Three men were lounging by the bunkhouse, flicking sidelong glances across at the wagon, conversing in low voices. They were rough, unshaven men, two of them heavy-set, wearing Union cavalry pants and holding tin cups as if they'd been interrupted in the middle of breakfast. The other was long and lean, clad in denim shirts and pants. All three men wore their weapons in tied-down holsters.

Not ranch hands, then. Jayhawkers. With the three men at the river, that made five in all – four left alive. Certain to be more somewhere. But what were they doing here? Renegades rode in, looted and burned, rode out. But for some reason this band was staying in the one place.

Close to the wagon another man stood tall alongside a big bay horse, and again Rivers noticed crusted dried blood, this on the horse's left flank. Although all the tall gunman's attention was fixed on the old man charging down the path, something alerted him to Rivers's approach. He half turned, and Rivers found himself gazing into strangely colourless eyes set in a lean, scarred face. For an instant both the man's gloved hands dropped to the .45s jutting from greased holsters, and Charlie Rivers braced himself for action.

Then a voice called, 'Later, Zac,' and Rivers's gaze snapped towards a slender man seated lazily astride a lean buckskin. Dark eyes glittered. Teeth gleamed white under a sweeping black moustache. Silver decorations shone on a fancy vest. And for a third time Charlie Rivers found his eyes drawn by blood, for this man's left leg had been recently injured and Rivers recalled watching the charging bandits from the knoll, his own shot followed by a yell of pain. . . . The bay and the buckskin carrying their riders alongside the still form by the river. . . .

Then Sam Wallace was confronting the man with the scarred face, bunched fists on bony hips as he roared, 'All right, you brought her home to me and I'm grateful. But who the hell killed my girl, Slaughter! If it was you, by God, reputation or no reputation I'll shoot you down like a dog.'

'Cool down, Wallace. It ain't like that.'

'Then how is it? Where did you find her? Goddammit, it's barely ten in the morning.'

The tall man shrugged. 'She rode out. Three of us rode after her. For her safety.'

'Hah!' The powerful rancher's voice was scathing, his eyes flashing fire. 'Going for the law, that's why. You had to stop her, or despite what I say your game would be over, finished.'

'Wallace, take a good look at my horse, and Blade Quatro's leg,' Slaughter said patiently. 'Your girl was unarmed. Quatro got that wound protecting her from the killers. A foot higher, the bullet that scarred my bay would've snapped my spine.'

Judas Priest! Charlie Rivers thought, and he shifted in the saddle, his eyes narrowing at the man's audacity.

Conflicting emotions were chasing each other across the rancher's granite countenance. His eyes wandered uncertainly, drifted with the merest flicker of interest past Charlie Rivers, finally settled on the man on the buckskin horse.

'What three rode after her?' he said, and now there was a different kind of tension in his voice. 'You, Blade Quatro, what the hell's he talking about?'

'Me and Slaughter, and Bart Hackett,' Quatro said. 'Bart took one in the chest, never made it back.'

Well, Charlie Rivers thought, that part at least can't be contradicted. He eased his horse forwards, swung out of the saddle and tied up at the rail. As he did so he glanced about him, noticed that a couple of the men from the bunkhouse had moved towards the wagon. Half-listening to the angry words being tossed back and forth, they were eyeing him with suspicion and edging closer.

At the same time the lean gunman who went by the name of Slaughter had gradually edged away from Wallace and was now almost close enough to reach out and touch Rivers's horse.

'Maybe they're tellin' the truth, Pa,' the young man said firmly. 'I know it don't make any kind of sense, but why else would they be all shot up, Hackett dead. . . ?' His hand settled placatingly on the big rancher's shoulder, and was at once roughly shaken off.

'Damn right it doesn't make sense,' Wallace

snarled, 'any more than my own son bringing this unsavoury bunch of renegades here in the first place makes sense. All I know is your stupidity – and I'm reluctant to concede that's all it is – is about to line these bandits' pockets with my hard-earned cash—'

'Shut up, Wallace!' Quatro growled, flicking a glance at Rivers.

At the same time the young man's mocking laugh rang out. 'My stupidity – and your cash? Hell, Pa, truth be told you're no better than the men that tried to save Jean—'

The rancher's bony hand flashed in the sunlight as he swung it backhand. The noise of his bunched knuckles striking his son's face was like the crack of a whip. The young man's head rocked. Every man watching could see the dead girl's blood staining his cheek. For an instant there was a strained silence. Then, his face twisted with contempt, Wallace turned again to the man called Slaughter.

'All right,' he said in a voice grown suddenly weary, 'if it wasn't you – who did kill Jean?'

'Strangers,' said Blade Quatro, and saddle leather creaked as he eased down off the buckskin and limped torwards Charlie Rivers. 'Ain't you noticed, Sam? There's so much senseless arguin' goin' on nobody's got around to askin' this feller what he's doin' on Running Irons property.'

FOUR

'You ride in with the body of Jeannie Wallace, spend the next half hour chewin' the fat with Blade Quatro and Zac Slaughter – then expect me to believe you not only had nothing to do with the killing, but you ain't set eyes on those two damn jayhawkers before today.'

'My word on it,' Rockwell Lane said. 'Now would you mind pointing that shotgun someplace else while we get this settled?'

'Haw!' The barked laugh was contemptuous, the big man's eyes chilling in their intent. Without shifting them or the shotgun from Rockwell Lane he said, 'Settlin' it's easy. You got a good strong rope handy, Blue?'

'Back off, Dave,' the ostler said brusquely. 'Ain't no trees in Concho Flats, nor no scaffold – and no goddamn law to convict this feller. Either you blow him in half with that Greener, or cool down and do some listenin'.'

'I'll hang around while you make your mind up,' the undertaker drawled, 'if you'll pardon my care-

44

less use of words.' He grinned apologetically at Lane. 'I was born lazy. Can't see the sense makin' two trips to the cemetery when one'll do.'

'There'll be no planting,' Lane said. He looked steadily at the irate storekeeper, and said quietly, 'You heard us discussin' a dead man. That means I rode in with two bodies, not one.'

'Hackett,' the lofty undertaker said, nodding confirmation. 'Took a bullet in the chest.'

'All that means is Jean put up a good fight.'

'No.' The ostler shook his head firmly. 'You know she don't carry a gun, Dave.' He cocked a shrewd eye at Lane, then said, 'This feller rode in from the east side of town. If he's come from the Concho that means Jean Wallace was already ten miles from home before the sun was all the way up. Why would that be?'

'I already know where she was, and what she was trying to do. I also know what stopped her.' The shotgun jerked alarmingly at Rockwell Lane, and he eyed the storekeeper's white knuckles and said softly, 'Go easy with that gun, feller, before another man dies.'

'Ain't nobody dyin' in my stable,' the ostler said bluntly. 'If you two fellers've got something to thrash out, do it over at the saloon while I tend to this fine horse. You, Lije, go dig Hackett's grave.'

That said, the little man turned his back on them and led Lane's horse down the dim, cool runway.

The undertaker shrugged, and said somewhat sadly to Rockwell Lane, 'I ain't given up on you –

but I guess your time ain't come.' With a mournful grin he swung about and walked out into the sunlit square. Seconds later, the two men locked at either end of the loaded and cocked shotgun heard the receding rattle of the hearse.

'Blue's talking sense,' Lane said quietly. 'I don't know what Zac Slaughter told you. Seems like you wouldn't be holding that gun on me if he hadn't come up with a logical explanation for Hackett's death, the blood on his own horse, Quatro's holed leg. But even you must know there's two sides to any story. Before you do something you'll regret, I think you should listen to mine.'

He gazed squarely into the storekeeper's eyes, saw the anger cooling, the frown that told of confusion and the beginnings of doubt. He went on, 'I'm gettin' kinda stiff standing here, so why don't we do what Blue says and walk across the square? With that gun on me I ain't going nowhere. . . .'

The store owner's jaw muscles bunched. Then he let a breath go explosively, waggled the shotgun and said, 'Move out. Walk in a straight line. You pull any tricks there'll be one almighty bang. You won't even hear it, but wherever he is Lije Coombs'll lift his head and realize your time has come.'

The town was coming awake like a weary old man whose sleep has been ruined by bad dreams. A stocky man in worn range garb came out of the café next to the bank, spat, settled his hat on his head, looked across with little interest at the two men linked by a shotgun, then climbed onto his pony and rode away. A slim woman in a calico dress splashed the contents of a bucket along the length of a gallery fronting what Lane guessed was a rooming house, and began brushing away the soapy water while occasionally tossing back her long hair and using the movement to throw inquisitive looks sideways at the two men marching across the square.

And outside a building marked 'Guns and Ammunition', two men in Union cavalry pants ignored what was going on as they chatted to a man in an oil-streaked apron who leaned in the doorway showing off a brand new, gleaming Winchester.

Then the shotgun nudged Rockwell Lane's spine. He had time to note that two fresh horses were at the hitch rail. One of them flicked its tail as he passed, then his boots were clattering on wood and he and the man holding the Greener found relief from the hot sun under the shade of the saloon's overhang.

Rockwell Lane thrust through the swing doors, was greeted by the same stale odours, saw the same barman standing in front of the mirror behind the same bar and told himself that walking around in circles was surely one way of driving himself crazy.

What it wouldn't do was clear up the motive that lay behind the girl's murder, or the mystery of the whereabouts of Jake Arkle who, it appeared, could be in two places at the same time.

'Two beers, Mick.'

The storekeeper's words fell dull and lifeless in the empty, silent room. He nodded curtly to Reilly and, as Lane hooked a chair and straddled it with his back to the door, he placed the Greener carefully on the table and sat down.

'My name's Dave Wilson. I run the general store. Feller owns the stable is Blue Hills. Lije Coombs is the man anxious to dig your grave. I guess you've met Mick Reilly.' He shook his head. 'I don't know why the hell I'm telling you all this. . . .'

'A short walk does a man good. You can smell a rat, Dave, same as any man with enough brains to rest his hat on.'

'You're a long way from being in the clear, Mister . . .'

'Rockwell Lane,' Lane said, and for a fleeting moment wondered if he should tell this man about the star set in a silver circle that both he and Charlie Rivers kept tucked away in their money belts, settle this once and for all by declaring himself as a Texas Ranger.

In the ten years he had been a ranger he had found keeping his authority secret for the longest possible time usually worked out best. But he had long known that this tendency stemmed from an inherent caution. When Indians were the most likely prowlers around the family farm on the Canadian, he had learned to stay close to the house when the best he could do in any case was a fast crawl across the dusty yard.

That caution had stayed with him through school, though not to the extent of saving him many bloody noses. And when both his parents had been slaughtered in a raid by marauding Cheyenne – so worn out with work they had ignored the barking of the family dog – it had been his caution that saved his life: where other youngsters might have panicked, and run, young Rockwell Lane burrowed deep into the sweet-smelling hay in the barn and didn't poke his head out until the posse were thundering down the rise.

The moment passed in a token silent debate, with the usual outcome. Caution won the day. The star set in the silver circle stayed out of sight. Mick arrived with two glasses of beer. Dave Wilson took a long drink, then set down his glass.

'Call it brains, call it instinct.' He pursed his lips, took time to watch his forefinger rub absently at the butt of the Greener. When he looked up he said quietly, 'What Zac Slaughter told me was him, Blade Quatro and Hackett ran into trouble over on the Concho when they caught two fellers gunning down Jean Wallace. He pointed no finger, but we both knew you'd just ridden in and he told me to think about it, work things out.'

'I guess that's one way of building suspicion,' Lane acknowledged.

'There's enough of it about since Arkle appeared on the scene,' Wilson said, and Lane felt himself go still at yet another mention of the familiar name. Without commenting he raised an eyebrow and waited.

Then Wilson sighed. 'Hell, what was I to believe? Hackett was dead, Quatro'd taken a slug, Slaughter's bay was bullet scarred. Jeannie Wallace was a tough kid, but we're talkin' about three grown men, rene-gades. . . .'

'And there was me, in one piece, parading the bodies like I'd done something to be proud of.'

Wilson laughed shortly. 'Put that way,' he said, 'I come out of it looking like the back end of a horse.'

Changing tack, Lane said, 'Jean Wallace. She'd be the daughter of Sam Wallace?'

'You know him?'

'Know of him. What I heard, he came from some-where back east with a pile of money he'd made, used it to buy and stock a ranch and make even more.'

Wilson nodded. 'That's about it. Which makes it all the more difficult to understand why he's takin' what's happenin' lying down.'

From across the square a bucket clattered. A woman's voice yelled what Lane thought might be 'Lije'. One of the horses at the hitch rail blew softly, as if in greeting. A man spoke quietly.

Behind the bar Mick Reilly raised the glass he was polishing, squinted through it at the sun shafting through the window and said, 'Even big men have skeletons in the cupboard, Dave.'

Dave Wilson frowned. 'You mean Arkle knows something that gives him a stranglehold on Wall-ace?'

'Must be something. For sure Wallace ain't scared of that outlaw,' Reilly said.

'So,' Rockwell Lane said, 'what exactly is it Arkle's doing?'

'What he's doing,' Wilson said bitterly, 'is round-ing up maybe two thousand head of Wallace's prime beef with the intention of driving to wherever the hell he can get the best price.'

Lane frowned. 'Renegades – working for a living?'

Mick Reilly's laughter was a deep, humourless bark. 'In the only way they know how, Rockwell: they point a gun, and Wallace's punchers do the job they're paid for.'

Lane sipped his beer. He thought that this was one crazy situation; one that from the start had made little sense. From what Wilson had told him it now seemed certain that Jean Wallace had been heading for San Angelo with some wild idea of getting the law on her side. But if that was the case, she would have been acting against the wishes of her father who, it seemed, was about to let armed rene-gades drive his herds to the cattle yards.

'If Wallace's crew's involved,' he mused aloud, 'it's with the old man's consent. Guns wouldn't hold them. So, in the eyes of the law, Wallace is giving away his beef of his own free will.'

He drained his beer, listened to the thud of boots on the plankwalk, said softly, 'What's your stake in this, Wilson?'

Dave Wilson glared. 'I run a store. What the hell d'you think happens to Concho Flats if Wallace goes under? He keeps his capital in the bank – and over the years that's built up into a tidy sum – but the profit those renegades make selling his cattle ain't going to end up there.' He shook his head angrily. 'But there's also friendship. Wallace is well liked, friendly with the man owns the bank – well, he would be – serves on what passes for a town council with him and a couple more of us. There's been talk of helping him, though so far he ain't made a complaint. My idea is—'

'Your idea ain't worth a lead peso, Wilson!'

The words were growled from the doorway. Turning his head, Lane saw the two men who had been standing talking to the gunsmith. They were standing just inside the swing doors. He was aware of movement behind the bar as Mick Reilly flipped the cloth onto his broad shoulder and put down the glass; felt the table dip as Dave Wilson's hands came down on it and he scooped up the Greener as he rose from his chair.

'Arkle's men?' Wilson's voice was harsh, contemptuous, as he turned towards the door. 'If you've ridden all this way to tell me that you've wasted your time—'

'The telling's all done.' The taller man had a seamed face ingrained with dirt, and unkempt greying hair. He wore a shabby black hat, held the gleaming new rifle low in one hand. His partner was short and lean, looked light enough to be blown away by a mild breeze. He was wearing two tied-down .45s, had drifted lazily through the shaft of sunlight and now stood where he could watch Wilson and Lane, and keep an eye on Mick Reilly.

Caught cold, Lane thought grimly. And feeling

exposed and helpless with his back to the older gunman he let his eyes slant towards the bar, saw that Mick Reilly's hands had slipped out of sight.

'Jake Arkle reckons we've done enough telling,' the tall gunman went on. 'He's decided you need teaching a final lesson.'

Wilson's mocking grin left his eyes as cold as ice. Deliberately easing back the Greener's hammers he said softly, 'Is that why you're playing with that new toy?'

'What, this purty thing?' The tall man frowned as if puzzled. He held the rifle out sideways, lifted it high as if it was the first time he had seen it, turned it slowly in his hands so that the sun's rays were reflected in the polished wood and a dazzling sliver of light streaked across the floor then floated high to hit the bar mirror and bounce back into Rockwell Lane's eyes. . . .

Almost casually, the short man made a fast right hand draw and shot Dave Wilson in the chest. At the same time the tall man flipped the Winchester down and a slug splintered the surface of the bar in front of Mike Reilly.

Grunting deep in his throat, Wilson dropped the shotgun. He clutched at his chest and fell backwards. The table's legs splintered. Wilson slid as the top tilted, flopped heavily to the floor.

Rockwell Lane kicked sideways out of his chair. He hit the floor and rolled clear, clawing for his six-gun. A red blob danced before his eyes from the piercing, reflected light. For an instant only he squeezed them tight shut in an effort to clear his vision. His entire body prickled in anticipation of the bullet that would end his life.

When he opened his eyes the tall gunman had not moved, the wisp of a man had shifted his pistol to cover Reilly.

A harsh laugh rang out. A second shot from the Winchester drove stinging splinters into Lane's face. A third tore the pistol from his hand. A fourth smashed the stock of the cocked Greener. The violent shock released the hammers. Both barrels fired with a deafening roar. From a foot away, the powerful charges of buckshot blasted a gaping hole in Wilson's side. Blood splattered the front of the bar, stained the motionless Reilly's white apron with ugly red blotches.

Slowly, carefully, Rockwell came to his knees, climbed to his feet. The stink of gunpowder filled the room. Smoke drifted in the slanting sunlight. Above the ringing in his ears he could hear men shouting, the rattle of a wagon.

Mick Reilly was swearing softly, using the cloth to wipe Dave Wilson's blood from his face.

'Now that,' the tall man said approvingly as he hefted the smoking Winchester, 'is what I call a damn fine rifle.'

FIVE

'The man I rode in to see is Sam Wallace,' Charlie Rivers said.

His words caused the limping man with the sweeping moustache to frown, and hesitate, and Rivers quickly stepped away from his horse and around the rail. Deliberately avoiding eye contact with the two jayhawkers he now knew as Quatro and Slaughter, he walked over to face the big rancher.

'Can we step inside, Sir?'

He looked into penetrating grey eyes that were narrowed against a potent mixture of confusion and anger, saw in them, behind that naked emotion, a sudden stirring of interest and beyond that, deeper still, a small spark in the depths that might perhaps have been the birth of hope.

'You ask that, knowing my daughter's lying in there, shot dead?'

'I've been listening.' Rivers nodded gravely. 'It sounds as if a couple of these men believe I was involved. I'd like to straighten that out.'

'Damn right we've got our suspicions,' Zac

Slaughter declared loudly. 'Another feller rode into Concho Flats. Brought in the two bodies, belly-down. . . .' His glance was swift as he saw the old man visibly wince, and pressing home the point he went on, 'Two men did the shooting down at the Concho, Wallace. Within a couple of hours, two strangers turn up – in different places, sure, but the last thing you need is strangers snoopin' around.'

'Got an army-issue Spencer in his saddle boot,' Blade Quatro pointed out. 'I got me a feeling if that slug had stayed in my leg 'stead of rippin' through it would've been a .52.'

'Pointless waste of words,' Sam Wallace snapped. 'And in case it slipped your mind, Jake Arkle may be running most other things around here but I'm still boss in my own home.'

He jerked his head at Rivers and stomped back towards the house and up the steps onto the gallery. Rivers followed, conscious of the dark young man falling in behind him and the two renegades reluctantly drifting away.

The gallery with its overhang shaded the windows, and the big room was spacious and cool. The floors were scattered with rugs, there was comfortable seating, dark sideboards and an elegant chiffonier, and heavy oil paintings created an air of opulence. The fireplace was built from massive blocks of stone, and Rivers recalled Rockwell Lane telling him that this man was a Virginian who had come west and made a fortune.

Made his cash in the West – or brought it with him? Rivers wondered. Then his eyes settled on the well-stuffed settee in the shadows, the long shape upon it covered by a white sheet, and again he tried to imagine why three men would set out to kill a girl in cold blood. . . .

He swept his hat off, stood patiently with it in his hands.

'All right, let's hear it,' Sam Wallace said. He'd crossed to take a humidor off the dresser, and was now lighting a fat cigar, puffing clouds of rich, blue smoke. 'What's so important you need to step inside my house before talking about it?'

'My life,' Rivers said.

Sam Wallace laughed shortly, jabbed the air with the cigar. 'Don't take me for a fool, young feller. Those two jayhawkers're blind to the obvious. My guess is you could take 'em both without raisin' a sweat.' He puffed at the cigar, glanced across at his son standing stiff and silent by the cold grate, then turned back to Rivers and said, 'Let me put it another way, dig a mite deeper. Were you over at the Concho when my girl was killed?'

Rivers pondered this for a few seconds, running his hat brim through his fingers, then said soberly, 'Let me answer one question with another. You said this feller's stupidity,' he nodded towards the watching man, 'is about to fill these renegades' pockets with your cash. How?'

Wallace grunted. 'Vern, my son. He fought on the wrong side during the war, allowed drinking cronies of his to get wind of a fortune in cattle.'

'Pa, you know it would have been wrong to enlist with the Confederacy,' Vern Wallace blurted. 'Hell, we're Virginians—'

'Were!' Sam Wallace shot back, jaw bulging. 'For the past ten years you and me've been Texans, boy. When we up and left Virginia, I *finished* with the Union.'

'You were *forced* to leave,' Vern Wallace accused. He had moved away from the stone grate and was standing confronting his father. His fists were clenched. The ugly bruise on his cheek was shiny in the weak light. 'We both know why you came to this godforsaken hole. It was to save your skin, but it killed ma, now it's killed Jean.'

'If anybody killed my daughter,' Sam Wallace said hoarsely, 'it was you, Vernon Wallace – and may God strike you down for it!'

The air quivered with tension. The two men glared at each other across the room, jaws thrust out, eyes blazing. They were engaged in a brutal confrontation within touching distance of the dead girl, wrangling furiously – and pointlessly – over which of them had caused her death. Yet it seemed to Charlie Rivers that poor Jean Wallace was not the issue. Maybe her dying – or the manner of it – had brought matters to a head, but the almost palpable hatred quivering between the middle-aged man and his young son was deep-rooted. And Rivers caught himself wondering why a forced exit from Virginia had saved big Sam Wallace's skin. . . .

Then Vernon Wallace took a deep breath, deliberately flexed his fingers. 'I'll check on the roundup,' he gritted, and turned to brush past Charlie Rivers. His boots pounded across the gallery, and as he ran down the steps he could be heard shouting for Zac Slaughter.

Sam Wallace stared down at his cigar. It was a crushed brown mess of shredded tobacco in his fist. Angrily he tossed the fragments onto the cold logs in the grate, and turned to look challengingly at Rivers.

'You represent the law?'

'Let's just say I understand enough about men who operate outside it to know these jayhawkers couldn't hang around without your say-so. The war's been over a year, maybe your son did let something slip when he was drinking with Arkle—'

'*Damn* Arkle!'

Rivers put his hat on, said quietly, 'Sure, I'll gladly drink to that. How long's he been here, Wallace?'

'None of your damn business!' The tetchy rancher narrowed his eyes, muttered something unintelligible, and said grudgingly, 'Rode in five, six days ago. Slaughter and the rest of those damned outlaws arrived the week before that. My guess is Slaughter or Quatro sent for Arkle, telegraph from San Angelo to wherever the hell he was.'

Rivers nodded, thinking of the black-eyed Mexican girl in the bar in Santa Fe, the gold double eagle gleaming between her pearly teeth. 'Yeah, that just about adds up.'

Wallace looked at him sharply. Then he frowned, shook his head. 'Don't know enough about you,' he said, apropos of nothing at all. 'Can't take the chance. . . .'

'Yeah, well,' Rivers said, walking out onto the gallery. 'What I came for was to ask for a job. But I guess my face wouldn't fit.'

'For one reason or another,' Sam Wallace said from the door and, though puzzled, for a moment Rivers thought he detected a note of regret.

Then he was outside in the dust and the heat. The wagon that had carried Jean Wallace's body had been moved down the sloping yard and was standing in the open doorway of the barn. Quatro was talking to Vern Wallace, watching him unhitch the horse. Zac Slaughter was making for the bunkhouse where the lean man in denims had a saddle over a rail, cleaning it and watching the tall gunman's approach.

Making like they run the place, Rivers thought as he mounted up – and Wallace is letting them do it. With those thoughts to occupy his mind he clicked his tongue, and with a shake of the reins he wheeled away from the ranch house and cantered up the slope towards the pines and, beyond that, the town of Concho Flats.

'Follow him,' Zac Slaughter said.

Tag Phillips nodded. 'But don't let him know.'

'That don't matter. He's already seen you, and if he's making for Concho Flats I want you to get close.'

'How close?'

Slaughter grinned. 'Don't hurt him. If he meets up with a tall, dark hombre, wide-spaced eyes, black hat, silver buckle and tip on the band – listen in if that's possible, ride back, let me know what went on.'

'Tall, dark. Southwesterner.' The lean man nodded. 'Consider it done, Zac.'

He hoisted the saddle and ambled off across the yard, lifted the gate bars and went into the corral. Five minutes later he emerged atop a frisky sorrel and rode up the hill in a cloud of dust.

SIX

By midday the sun was a searing orb directly over the naked expanse of dust that was Concho Flats's town square, the fickle breeze that had earlier had sport with the tumbleweed and greeted Rockwell Lane with its dust-larded balm now a wistful memory.

The two renegade gunmen had faded from the saloon almost as fast as the gunsmoke, and Lane assumed they had left town. A genuinely distressed Lije Coombs had taken a deep, bracing swig from a dented silver hip flask, then carted away Dave Wilson's body in the gleaming hearse. Rockwell Lane had recovered his .45, examined the chipped butt, then wandered across to the gunsmith to ask one question and get the answer he expected: the tall gunman with dirty grey hair had bought the new Winchester by ramming the muzzle of his .45 under the gunsmith's chin, then cocking the action.

Mick Reilly spent the first half hour after the shooting kicking himself because he'd been too slow getting the shotgun up from behind the bar to save Wilson, the second moaning about his splintered bar and mopping up blood. As the morning wore on several men drifted in to wash the dust from their throats, and loaf. Big Mick did the only thing he could under the circumstances: he served glasses of warm beer, proudly displaying the dried blood splashed across the front of his apron and telling and re-telling the tale.

Rockwell Lane ended up at a table by the window in the nearby café. There, over fried beef and pota- toes and mugs of hot black coffee, he gazed out over the baking square and added up what he knew – and surmised – while exercising his jaw muscles on what felt like sun-dried leather.

According to Dave Wilson, Lane recalled, members of the Concho Flats town council were ready to act to prevent what was happening to Sam Wallace. Trouble was, it appeared that what was happening – namely, the gather and ultimate sale of his cattle by renegades – was being done with Wallace's consent.

As he prised a piece of stringy meat out of a tooth and washed it down with hot coffee, Lane admitted that one possible answer was that everything was above board. Sam Wallace had hired the renegades as cow-punchers: they'd drive his cattle to market, hand over the cash and collect their wages.

But there were two visible cracks in that cosy picture. The first was the death of Jean Wallace. The second was the rumoured presence of Jake Arkle.

The renegade was possibly one of the most devi- ous, cold-blooded killers Rockwell Lane had ever had the misfortune to pursue. But where Arkle was at a disadvantage was in being the latest in a very long line of such ruthless bandits. Familiarity had not bred contempt in Lane, but a healthy caution (well, he'd already had that!), and along with it the ranger had amassed a vast store of experience in the ways of the nefarious armed gentlemen who roamed the West.

If Arkle was at the Running Irons, he was not there to punch cows!

The café door clicked open, interrupting Lane's thoughts, and a florid man in a dark business suit powdered with dust walked in, nodded to the counter hand, then came across to Lane.

'Mind if I join you?'

'Be a pleasure,' Lane said. 'Anything that stops me going crazy trying to work out the impossible is welcome.'

'Know the feeling.' The big man sat down heavily, shot his cuffs and extended a plump hand. 'Alan Moffatt,' he said. 'I own the bank.'

'Well, now.' Lane shoved away the greasy plate and sat back. 'My name's Rockwell Lane. And you're a town council member—'

'Chairman.' Moffatt beamed importantly, his prominent eyes shining with pride.

'Sure. And you and your fellow councillors are about to help old Sam Wallace.'

'What with?'

'That,' Rockwell Lane said, 'is what's drivin' me crazy.'

He sipped his coffee, and watched as a steaming plate was dumped in front of the bank manager and the perspiring official used a blunt knife to cut a bite-sized chunk of meat. As the big man began methodically masticating Lane met his eyes and said, 'For some reason, Sam Wallace is being robbed, but keeping his mouth tight shut. Jean Wallace couldn't go along with that. Her efforts to recruit some law got her killed.'

He held up his hand as the bank manager worked the soggy meat into his cheek and opened his mouth as if to speak. 'Enough people have mentioned a feller called Jake Arkle for me to believe he's involved,' Lane continued. 'That sorta settles matters. Arkle's a known criminal.'

Moffatt swallowed with a visible effort and said, 'Not wanting to argue but merely offering a word of caution, criminals do occasionally change their ways, Mister Lane.'

'And cows get rustled, Mister Moffatt, but not too often with their owners' consent.'

'Noooo. . . . And I must admit that I'm concerned. . . .'

Which, if it was meant to impress Lane, did no such thing, for the look he saw in the banker's eyes was suggesting an entirely different sentiment.

'Wallace worth a packet?'

'Let's say that, for me – and that also means the town's well-being – banking would be less profitable if Wallace . . . if he suffered a setback.'

'So?'

Moffatt shrugged massively, then sighed and pushed away his meal. 'There's no law officer in Concho Flats, Mister Lane – and if you are thinking of some form of organized vigilante group, how many willing, able bodied men have you seen during your short stay?'

'Not too many,' Lane admitted, 'and their numbers 're already being whittled away by said criminal element.'

Moffatt ordered coffee and lit a store-bought cigarette, his eyes speculative. 'You, now,' he said, clearing his throat. 'What brings you to town, Mister Lane?'

'Passing through.' Lane smiled amiably. 'Got a partner rode out looking for a ridin' job out the Running Irons – but I guess from what I've pieced together about the situation he'll be back before dark.'

'Two of you. . . . And there's Blue Hills, the ostler, Lije Coombs – I know for a fact he's been affected by the death of Wilson. . . .'

'By your own admission that's sort of a rag-tag army to go up against a bunch of wild jayhawkers, Moffatt.'

'I'm a bank manager, Lane,' Moffatt said, the thoughtful deliberation still in his eyes. 'You have the advantage over me. I do, of course, understand a man's reluctance to divulge too many secrets . . . but where violence is concerned perhaps you are more . . . experienced?'

'Could be,' Lane said unhelpfully as he pushed

back his chair. 'Assuming you mean in an enthusiastic, amateur kind of way.'

He left the bank manager with his coffee and cigarette and an increasingly disturbed expression on his red face, settled his black hat on his head and wandered out into the midday heat. As he did so a rider cantered past the shacks on the edge of town, heading in, and suddenly Rockwell Lane was grinning as he lengthened his stride and stretched out across the square to meet Charlie Rivers.

Charlie had slid out of his rig and was handing the reins to Blue Hills as Lane reached the livery stable. Lije Coombs was ankle deep in cool straw, lounging against the side of one of the stalls, the silver hip flask in his hand and a lugubrious expression on his long face.

'Journey wasted?'

Rivers took his time answering. First he spent some pleasant seconds stretching the kinks out of his joints while watching Blue Hills tend to his horse. Then he swept off his hat and slapped the dust off his clothes, all the while looking sideways at Lije Coombs. Finally, he said quietly, 'Sam Wallace and me spent all of ten minutes in the same room and still couldn't decide who was on which side.'

'The long ride back help to untangle your thoughts?'

'Nope. The man's lost a daughter, must know she was killed by the same men're about to steal his cows – but he don't do nothing.'

Lane sighed. 'I've been through this so many times I'm dizzy.' He watched Blue Hills stripping the hull from Rivers' horse, and quickly filled the ranger in on the ride into town, the encounter with Zac Slaughter and Blade Quatro, the subsequent killing of Dave Wilson by two more of the jayhawkers and the meeting with the bank manager. Drawing to a close, he said, 'D'you see Arkle out at the ranch?'

Rivers chuckled. 'You must be askin' all the wrong questions. That gets you another no.' He scratched his head, replaced his hat and said, 'But I guess you've already heard his name mentioned a few times, and I did find out Arkle got where he's at about six days ago – about a week after the main bunch. Wallace reckons he was sent for.'

Lane jutted his lip, nodding thoughtfully. 'That adds up, if we take it we was made fools of by that *señorita*.' He grinned ruefully. 'So, where is Arkle at?'

'Why don't you rephrase that one, friend?' Blue Hills said. He came back up the runway folding a saddle blanket, tossed it over a rail and said, 'Ask your pal if Jake Arkle's at the Running Irons.'

Lane cocked an eyebrow. 'Is he?'

Rivers shook his head. 'Nope.'

'See, now you've got something you can get your teeth into,' Blue Hills said. 'You know for sure where he isn't at. It's called a process of elimination – but, hell, you two lawmen should know all about that.'

'Made damn sure they know just about everything else,' the tall, gaunt, frock-coated undertaker said with a dignity that might have come out of the silver flask. 'They've bin eyeing the both of us ever since that skinny little ranger rode in.'

'Compared to you I may be a mite on the short side,' Charlie Rivers said indignantly, 'but I ain't never been called—'

'Maybe,' Rockwell Lane cut in sharply, 'we'd all better step inside your office, Blue.'

'Don't look behind you,' the chirpy little ostler said, 'but I think maybe you're right.'

He jerked a thumb towards the rickety office structure, and as the two rangers stepped quickly inside and pushed the door to Lane heard the slowing rattle of hooves and the soft blowing that told of a horseman pulling into the stable.

'Anyone follow you?' he asked softly.

'Didn't look, too busy tryin' to figure out what the hell's goin' on.' Rivers squinted through the crack between the closed door and its misshapen frame, then nodded. 'Yeah, tall feller in denim, was by the Running Irons' bunkhouse when I rode out.'

They both waited impatiently, Lane with his back to the door, listening. A bridle jingled and boots scraped as the new arrival stepped down and handed over his horse. Lije Coombs belched, and begged everybody's pardon. There was the tinkle of a coin, a soft curse. Then footsteps, receding. Saddle leather creaked, straw rustled, a horse nickered.

'Comin',' Charlie Rivers grunted, and Lane stepped away from the door as Blue Hills entered the office followed by the lofty Lije Coombs.

'Careful with the delicate china,' Hills remarked, his keen blue eyes unreadable. He sat down by the littered desk in the only chair, moved a battered coffee pot and an old tin cup, swept a pile of papers to one side and sent a couple of worn horseshoes ringing to the floor. Rivers hiked one haunch onto the edge of the desk, put his back up against the wall. Lije Coombs stood tall against the door, looking for all the world like a long black coat hanging from one of the pegs.

Rockwell Lane hooked an empty wooden crate, sat down.

'All right,' he said. 'What gave us away?'

'Memory,' Blue Hills said with obvious satisfaction. 'Mine, not yours. I worked for a spell in Austin, five or six years back. Hung around, had me an idea rangering was the life for me until I got told I was about two feet too short,' He grinned. 'Rockwell Lane and Charlie Rivers – right?'

Lane met the ostler's bright blue eyes, nodded slowly. 'That feller rode in was a renegade. You kept your mouth shut.'

'And I ain't ashamed to say I shed a tear over Dave Wilson,' Lije Coombs said. 'That tell you enough about allegiances?'

'Big words comin' out of a little flask, Lije,' Blue Hills said with a faint smile, but his thoughts were elsewhere and he went on, 'Saw you talkin' to

Moffatt, Lane. D'you get a clear message about where his sympathies lie?'

'He beat around the bush some, but I got the impression he'd be happy to see those jayhawkers take Wallace's cattle.'

'You figured right. On the town council, he was the one voted we leave Sam to handle things his way.'

Rivers pulled out the makings, began fashioning a cigarette. His brow was furrowed. 'Wallace loses money. The bank loses money. The two men concerned don't bat an eyelid. Why?'

'Only one possible reason,' Blue Hills said.

Rockwell Lane nodded. 'Those two know something we don't.'

The door creaked as Coombs shifted his weight and slipped the silver flask into a deep pocket. 'Nobody ever did spend time digging into Sam Wallace's background,' he said.

'And according to Wallace himself,' Charlie Rivers said, cigarette poised, 'his son Vern brought this whole mess down on their heads.' He poked the cigarette between his lips, applied a match flame and trickled smoke. 'According to Vern, Wallace ain't no better than the men killed Jean.'

For a few minutes there was silence in the small office. Lije Coombs stepped away from the door and went poking about among the mildewed old saddles heaped against the back wall. Blue Hills accepted the makings from Rivers and began to build a cigarette. Through a haze of smoke Rivers did his

damndest to bore through Rockwell Lane's skull
with a fierce gaze and watch the workings of his
superior officer's mind. Though, in truth, he had
no need. Ever since the name of Arkle had been
linked to the Running Irons, he knew that once the
talking was out of the way there could only be one
possible course of action.

All that had for some time been crystal clear to
Charlie Rivers. In fact, he mused with an inward
smile, it frequently amazed him how old Rockwell
got to be captain with such slow thought processes.

As if he'd read Charlie Rivers's mind a damn sight
better than Rivers had read his, Rockwell Lane
finally broke the silence.

'What we've got to do,' the ranger captain said
firmly, 'is to quit dancin' *around* the main issue and
get the hell *on* with it. That issue bein', the appre-
hension and takin' into custody of one Jake Arkle.'

'After which,' Charlie Lane said happily, 'every
damn thing'll fall into place of its own accord.'

'But if we *don't* get on with it,' Lane continued,
warming to the subject and now addressing Blue
Hills and Lije Coombs, 'Alan Moffatt and his town
council – I take it that includes Sam Wallace? – are
going to discover some unsavoury truths. One being
I can't ever recall jayhawkers wasting time herding
cows. The second being nothing I've heard in
Concho Flats makes me believe this is going to be the
first time.'

'Is that supposed to tell us something?' Lije
Coombs asked, straightening his long frame from

inspecting the saddles, and dusting off his bony hands.

'Supposed to plant seeds, Lije,' Rockwell Lane said. 'When you go about your business, the heat of the sun'll make 'em sprout into ideas that'll show you where all of this is leading.'

'I'd better get outside, then,' Lije Coombs said. 'I could use some ideas to pass on to Alan Moffatt, shake him out of his intolerable complacency.'

As he rolled his tongue around the big words, he tapped the pocket containing his silver flask and winked at Blue Hills. Then, like a turkey stretching its neck, he eased his throat against his high wing collar and, with a lingering backward glance at the heaped leatherwear, he pulled open the door and ducked through the frame.

'Old Lije, he's got a room full of old saddles,' Hills explained. 'Fancies himself as a cowpoke, aims to impress Widow Logan who runs the roomin' house – though the only thing I've ever seen him ride is the seat of that hearse.'

'Maybe he'll get his chance to shine,' Lane said. 'Blue, you've been in Concho Flats five or six years, me and Charlie not that many hours. If Jake Arkle's got business at the Running Irons, but he ain't there and he ain't in town – where would you look?'

'Line cabin, out at Buffalo Ridge,' Hills said at once.

'Why there?'

Hills spread his hands. 'Ten miles from the ranch it's close enough to be within easy reach, far enough

to be out of the way. And if those renegades *are* planning on stealing beef, Wallace uses the next valley as
a natural corral.'

'Maybe that was their original intention,' Lane
conceded. 'War's been over a year, ranchers all over
Texas've begun driving cattle north to Kansas where
they can get fifty dollars a head. Best route from
here is to pick up the Chisholm Trail at Fort Worth.'
He shook his head doubtfully.

Charlie Rivers killed his cigarette and said quietly,
'If Arkle is at the cabin, it'll likely be the best, maybe
the only place to take him. Far as I could tell, the
rest of the renegades 're using the ranch bunkhouse.'

'How many are we up against, Charlie?'

'I saw three men, plus Slaughter and Quatro. It
was one of the three followed me in.'

'Add the two killed Dave Wilson, that makes
seven, plus Jake Arkle.' He turned to Hills. 'How
big's the cabin, Blue?'

Hills shook his head. 'Your pal's right. Most of
'em'll stay at the ranch.'

'Arkle, Slaughter and Quatro.' Lane rubbed the
broad line of his jaw. 'I can't swallow this cattle drive
theory. My guess is those three're planning something big, something they can easy handle on their
own – and adding up what we know about Sam
Wallace, it don't take a whole heap of intelligence to
figure out what that is.'

He raised an enquiring eyebrow at Blue Hills, saw
the slow nod of understanding. 'So if I was Arkle,'

Lane went on, 'while that little scheme's fermenting I'd leave one man at the ranch, sort of keeping an eye on the wild bunch at night. The other I'd keep with me at the cabin.'

He nodded slowly as the idea took shape in his mind. 'If we're lucky, we ride up to the cabin there'll be just two men to face. Arkle, and either Slaughter or Quatro.'

'Last time I saw such favourable odds,' Charlie Rivers reminisced, 'was when we hit that outlaw camp below Cloud Peak in the Bighorns, and—'

'Sure, Charlie,' Lane cut in, his dark eyes amused. He rose stiffly from the crate, yawned, and said to Blue Hills, 'You reckon you can have both horses ready about an hour before sunset?'

'We hit 'em after dark,' Rivers said, and nodded his approval.

The wiry little ostler dropped his cigarette, ground it under his boot, got to his feet. 'Sam Wallace and Alan Moffatt have been mighty indignant – and mighty certain – about what's going on at the Running Irons. You sure you know what you're doing, Lane?'

Rockwell Lane nodded. 'I'm getting there, Blue. I don't know about indignant – I truly believe that's an act – but Sam Wallace and Moffatt are certain because that's what they believe. They believe it because, when Vern Wallace put them up to it, Slaughter and Quatro set out to steal cattle and made no secret of it. But after maybe a week of backbreaking work, they sent for Arkle – because, plumb tired of sweat and dust and bawling long-horns, one or both of them had come up with a better idea. . . .'

SEVEN

Beyond the Running Irons, some ten miles ride north and west through rolling grassland in the widening fork of the North and Middle Conchos, a stout line cabin built from heavy logs was set high at the back of a clearing on the edge of woods that lay like a dark buffalo pelt along the side of a hill.

On the other side of the crest a wide, closed valley had been temporarily fenced off at its open end, and it was from the top of the hill that the outlaw Jake Arkle spent half an hour in the late afternoon sun watching the activity through army field glasses.

Dust was a thin, dun cloud drifting the full length of the vast enclosure. The bellowing of cattle filled the air. Cow-punchers whooped and hollered and through the glasses the spread of the milling steers' mighty longhorns could be seen flashing as if polished in the sunlight.

Here it was that Sam Wallace's punchers were

penning the cattle they were rounding up for the benefit of Jake Arkle. He was an easterner, Arkle. The sight of hundreds, thousands of half-wild beasts and the cowboys circling them on nimble ponies never failed to stir the blood in his veins. So he lingered long, his mind often elsewhere, before turning his mount and threading his way through the timber and back to the cabin.

As he dismounted, off-saddled and set the horse loose in the small corral back of the cabin, the long, half-pleasurable minutes of romantic reverie had been banished from his mind and he allowed himself a small, twisted smile of satisfaction.

One part of a twin-pronged scheme, meticulously planned to turn Sam Wallace into a pauper and Jacob Benson Arkle once again into a very rich man, was progressing without a hitch.

The cabin was just big enough to hold a couple of bunks, a rickety pine table, two crude chairs and an iron stove. On the stove, strong coffee bubbled. Arkle lifted the pot, splashed the steaming black liquid into a cup and walked to the window.

He was expecting Blade Quatro and Zac Slaughter. Although patience had always been his strong point, the early morning trouble with Jean Wallace had hit hard. The cattle roundup was going well and his men were unlikely to find trouble on the drive north to Abilene, but the outcome of the second phase of his scheme to ruin Sam Wallace was still balanced on a knife edge.

More importantly, Arkle was cursing himself for

failing to grasp from Jean Wallace's increasing agitation that she was tired of watching her father eating crow, and had got it into her head to ride to San Angelo.

One more lapse like that could kill both ideas stone dead.

As he sipped the scalding coffee Arkle wondered edgily if the three men he'd sent after the girl had managed to cut her off, bring her back. He thought it unlikely they'd done it without one hell of a war of words. If she'd refused to be cowed, pressed on regardless of their threats – and, by heck, she was spirited enough – well . . .

Well nothing! Quatro and Slaughter could be relied on. Whatever needed doing, would have been done. But the smouldering anger wouldn't go away and, as he stepped to the open door, Arkle flung away the last of the coffee in a fit of temper and dragged the makings from his shirt pocket with fingers that trembled.

Though carrying a week's growth of dark beard and wearing a shabby blue shirt and faded cavalry pants, there was about Jake Arkle the unmistakable air of breeding. But beneath that manner, and in the pale blue eyes, there was a brittle hardness. Like many men, he had emerged from the bitter fighting of the Civil War apparently unchanged, but with all the instinctive beliefs in the inherent goodness of his fellow countrymen badly scarred. Unlike most of those other men, Arkle had been harbouring bitterness in his soul before the onset of war, and he had carried it with him and nurtured it for four long years.

As he trickled smoke, stowed away the tobacco sack and squinted his blue eyes to gaze off into the lengthening shadows stretching out towards the Running Irons, the memories of those past times were in Jake Arkle's mind. Yet again he marvelled how, in six years, his life had been ruined by one man's greed, and his own violent reactions to its effects. From the privileged position of heir to a sprawling Virginia estate, he had been transformed into an outlaw with his picture on Wanted dodgers across the West.

The Running Irons! Arkle laughed with genuine amusement. He had to hand it to Sam Wallace, the wily old thief sure had his tongue firmly in his cheek when he chose that name.

Two dots appeared out of the first faint tendrils of evening mist curling atop a distant rise, and Arkle grunted in satisfaction, and flicked away the cigarette. Fifteen minutes later the two gunmen rode up the slope, quickly unsaddled, put their horses in the corral and entered the cabin.

Arkle was seated at the table, head down, carefully oiling the mechanism of his old Henry repeater. He spread an oil-soaked cloth in the palm of his hand, closed his fist around the Henry's barrel and ran it up and down the smooth steel, while the two gunmen kicked the door shut and stacked their saddle-booted Winchesters in a corner.

When Arkle did glance up he stared pointedly at

Blade Quatro's leg, and said, 'All right, what the hell happened?'

Quatro was sitting on the bunk, gunbelt over the rail, injured leg stretched out. His black eyes glinted in the shadows.

'You must've known there was only one way of stopping that fiery little vixen,' he said, and Arkle swore softly.

Zac Slaughter shrugged carelessly, tossed his hat on the table. 'It's done, over with. She didn't make it as far as the San Angelo law, everything goes ahead as planned.'

'Somebody exacted a price.' Arkle was folding the rag, putting away the oil bottle. 'I see one man with a holed leg, a scarred horse outside – and I know damn well that gal never carried a gun.'

Slaughter met Arkle's intelligent gaze and said defensively, 'A couple of fellers on a knoll alongside the Concho saw what was going on. Hell, we didn't even see them until too late.'

'We got the girl,' Quatro said, 'But Hackett didn't make it.'

'Bart Hackett dead!'

There was fury in Jake Arkle's eyes and Quatro went on hurriedly, 'Sam Wallace is shoutin' his mouth off, threatenin' to blow Zac's head off if it was him killed Jean. . . .'

'Gettin' to sound like he ain't got much left to lose,' Zac Slaughter added. 'We don't move fast, Jake, he might figure to hell with it.'

'You're wrong,' Arkle said flatly. 'Sam Wallace

knows damn well the law gets wind of who he is he'll spend the rest of his life behind bars. He won't stop us taking those longhorns. Hell, why should he? He's got more money stashed in the Concho Flats bank than most of us've seen in one place.'

Zac Slaughter chuckled throatily. 'Yeah, Jake, all Sam's got to do is watch his longhorns disappear over the skyline, buy himself a fresh herd when the dust's settled and start all over.'

'Exceptin',' Quatro said, teeth flashing white under the sweeping black moustache, 'by the time the dust's settled old Sam won't *have* any cash in Concho Flats or any other bank.'

'Damn right he won't,' Jake Arkle said, his eyes glittering. 'No cows, no cash. Wiped out.' He looked away, probed the shadows piling up outside the window, and said distantly, 'It'll be his turn to twist at the pain . . . suffer the shame. . . .'

For a time that was the end of talk. Blade Quatro muttered softly through tight lips while he dressed his wound. Zac Slaughter unbuckled his gunbelt and hung it on the back of a chair, then set to clattering pots on the iron stove and starting thick slices of bacon sizzling in a mess of beans. The light swiftly faded. Jake Arkle scraped a match, lit the lamp and yellow light pooled on the earth floor, spilled out onto grass already sparkling with dew. A coyote howled, off in the hills. One of the horses snorted.

Inside the cabin there was something more than the pleasant night quiet of three men ending a long day, preparing to eat. There was tension; all three renegades felt it, were attuned to it as all such men are.

Blade Quatro was the one to break the silence.

'Jake, those two fellers, over at the Concho,' he said, as Slaughter handed him a steaming plate. 'I think they could be trouble.'

'How?' Arkle said. He was at the table, fork poised over his plate, his eyes ugly.

'One of 'em, a dark, lean *hombre*, rode into Concho Flats with the bodies of Hackett and the girl. The other turned up at the ranch, spoke to Wallace. Short, wiry, big shoulders. Hard as nails.'

'Jesus!' Arkle bit off a hunk of bacon, chewed mechanically, his eyes narrowed. Talking to himself he mumbled, 'Two of them, just happened to be at the Concho. Split up now, but still hanging around.' He tapped the plate agitatedly with his fork, eyes darting.

'Were split.' Slaughter shrugged uncomfortably, eased himself down onto the floor with his back against the wall. 'The wiry feller looked as if he was heading back to town. I put Tag Phillips on his tail.'

'Waste of time.' Arkle shoved his almost full plate away, drummed his fingers on the table, mind raking through the recent past. 'I got your wire in Santa Fe, sold the best horse I ever had to a breed heading home. Told a black-eyed Mex bitch in a *cantina* if two men came a-lookin' to sell 'em what she knew: the *gringo*, Jake Arkle, was riding west. Then I stole a lean, long-legged black devil built for speed, followed the Pecos hard clear to Mescalero Ridge, cut south-east. . . .'

'If that was them at the Concho they must have tailed the breed a couple of weeks, maybe caught him, took one look at his face and guessed what you'd done. . . .' Quatro's voice trailed off, one hand absently massaging his leg.

'Texas Rangers,' Arkle said flatly. 'It's them all right. Rockwell Lane and Charlie Rivers. Hell, they must've been on their way to Austin, cursing the fact they was empty handed, stopped off at the river and three hellions come ridin' out've the dawn, damn near give themselves up.'

'You're building a goddamn mountain out of a speck of dust, Jake,' Slaughter protested. He scraped his plate, sent it clattering towards the stove, angrily drove his knife deep into the dirt floor. 'They're here – but what can they do? Sam Wallace's own waddies're doing the gather and drive of their own free will and with Sam's blessing. And there ain't nobody but us three knows about the bank.'

'Not yet they don't.' Arkle tipped the chair back so that his bulk was over two creaking legs, ran thick fingers through his coarse black hair. 'But those two'll move fast – so we've gotta move faster.' He scratched his head, slammed the chair back down, came up out of it fast and began to pace back and forth.

'The cattle drive has to be halfway to the Red before we raid the bank,' Quatro said. 'Wallace'll only co-operate while he knows his cash is safe.'

'Can't take the risk of waiting.' Arkle stopped his pacing to peer out of the window. 'Besides, didn't I just tell you Sam Wallace'd sell his grandmother to keep his past secret?'

He swung around, his pale eyes glinting like steel. 'Here's what we do. We raid the bank tomorrow morning, soon's Moffatt opens up. We've got the cash, we go straight on through, ride like the devil's on our tail – now, ain't that the truth! The Bravo's 'bout 120 miles due south. Once across we can take our time, rest up for six months when we reach Nuevo Laredo.'

Slaughter nodded. 'It'll work. Cut the gather short, start the drive early. Wallace is settin' tight, waiting for things to happen. His rannies ain't been to town for more'n a week, ain't likely to go once they get word to move. Tag Phillips can put a man up in the pines south of the ranch. If anyone rides from town with news of the robbery, they can be stopped.'

'Sure.' Blade Quatro eased himself off the bed, tested his leg, grimaced. 'This'll've eased by morning. To get my hands on that cash I'd crawl over broken glass.'

Jake Arkle grinned savagely. The decision had taken all the weight from his shoulders. He flexed his shoulders, took a coat from a hook behind the door, shrugged into it and fastened it over his gunbelt.

'I'll take a ride over to the herd, tell Wallace's

straw boss the gather's over. Be bright moonlight shortly—'

'You there, in the cabin!'

EIGHT

'Left town,' Mick Reilly said. 'Saw you two come out of Blue's stable, hung around till you were over at the store then snuck over, got his mount and rode out the back way. Leastways, he never came out again.'

Charlie Rivers had asked what had happened to the tall man in denim who'd followed him in from the Running Irons. Rockwell Lane pulled a face at Reilly's answer.

'No more than I expected,' he said ruefully. 'Slaughter and Quatro have seen both of us, at different times. Now they'll know we're together. If Jake Arkle knows two rangers were hot on his heels at Sante Fe, it won't take him too long to work out what us two bein' here means.'

The two rangers, beer glasses in hands, were lounging with their backs to the bar in Reilly's Pleasure Palace. The last of the afternoon's sunlight slanted over a sleepy, three-man poker game. The piano's yellowed keys were being tinkled with skill and sadness by an enormous fat man with lank black hair whose rolled up shirt sleeves exposed the powerful arms of a blacksmith. Lije Coombs stood in bowed, dejected solitude at the end of the bar, listening to the music and nursing a whiskey, a mournful, thin man in a black suit.

'He offered his services,' Lane told Reilly with a faint smile. 'Didn't want to hurt his feelings, so I told him in those clothes we'd lose him in the dark.'

'My offer still stands,' the big saloon owner said seriously. 'Blackie Nelson tends bar when he ain't playing piano or shoeing horses. I won't be missed.'

'Just the opposite, Mick,' Lane said, 'and that's one reason why I can't take you along. You're so big *nobody'd* be able to miss you, and Lije has already buried one of his friends.'

'And the other reason?' Reilly asked resignedly.

'This is official ranger business that's got nothing to do with Sam Wallace. Jake Arkle was bad before he came to Concho Flats. Like Wallace he's an easterner who came out West. Difference is, Arkle was already treading the outlaw trail long before the war. Left a trail of murder and robbery as he rode through Kentucky, Missouri and into the Nations, earned himself an ugly reputation in those bloody years after Fort Sumpter. In the twelve months since Appomatox he's run wild with one bunch of jayhawkers or another. Most recently he's thought to have led a band murdered a ranching family north of Amarillo. First time me and Charlie've got close to him is when we picked up his trail in Santa Fe.'

'Blackie's always been after old Blue's stable,' Reilly said as Lane finished his tale. 'Blue's told him if he gets what he most wants out of life, Blackie can have the whole shebang for a song – exceptin', of course, those two thoroughbreds he keeps.' Reilly looked keenly at Lane. 'D'you know what it is Blue wants?'

'I know,' Lane said, recalling the pint-sized ostler's remarks about his spell in Austin. He shook his head. 'Thought he looked like he raced horses, first time I saw him.'

'He don't,' Reilly said. 'Blue sort of came into possession of those two blue grass beauties by default. The owner placed them in his care, then expired violently at the wrong end of a .45.'

Charlie Rivers turned to place his glass on the bar. 'Sun's almost down, Rocky,' he said, and Lane drained his glass. As Rivers headed for the door he said quietly to Reilly, 'If you can't ride with us you can keep your eyes open, Mick. Sooner or later Arkle's going to show his true colours. When he does you'll be needed here in town, and that shot-gun of yours'll come in useful. . . .' He nodded to the big bartender, and turned to follow Rivers.

The sun's dying rays were highlighting the glossy paintwork of Lije Coombs's hearse and transforming its wide windows into vast red mirrors as they headed across the wide square, their shadows long in the dust. The interior of the livery stable was dim and cool. Blue Hills emerged from the office as they stepped into the gloom. Their mounts, he confirmed, were saddled and ready by the wide rear entrance.

As he walked down the runway with them he said quietly, 'Ride north for a mile. You'll come up on the Concho right where there's a shallow ford under a stand of willows. Once across the river, veer towards the west. The moon'll come up in line with Buffalo Ridge. The cabin's in the lee of the eastern slope. Wallace's cow hands are holding the herd in the valley over the hill.'

'Too close for comfort,' Lane said thoughtfully as they reached the horses.

'Cow hands,' Charlie Rivers pointed out, 'not jayhawkers. Those renegades won't sleep rough when there's a bunkhouse within riding distance.'

'And if there is any shooting,' Blue Hills said, 'those rannies'll figure the jayhawkers're fighting amongst themselves, and bury their heads in their blankets.'

Rockwell Lane hesitated, hand on saddle. 'Blue,' he said gravely, 'there's no saying what'll happen tonight. Most likely things'll turn out fine. If they do, you'll see us ride in with one or more of those renegades. If that don't happen, and we ain't turned up by first light, would you go over to the bank for me and tell Alan Moffatt to expect trouble?'

'Soon's he opens the doors,' the ostler said vehemently. 'That ain't just Sam Wallace's cash he's holding for safe-keeping!'

Lane clapped the little ostler gratefully on the shoulder. Then, without wasting time, he swung into the saddle. Leather creaked alongside him as Rivers followed suit. Blue Hills faded into the shadows.

Then they were out of the stable and riding stirrup past the corral and through a wide alley that led them away from the square and out into rolling open countryside suffused with pink light from the sinking sun.

'You got a plan?' Charlie Rivers asked eventually, and Rockwell Lane's eyes shone as he glanced across at his fellow ranger.

'I don't aim to get killed,' he said, and Rivers chuckled.

'Yeah,' he said, 'that's about as far as I've figured it.'

They rode in silence for a while, each man appreciating the cooling evening breeze, half-listening to the gentle blowing of their mounts, the swish of grass, the occasional rattle of a loose stone. The air was rich with the scent of cooling sagebrush. A night-bird fluttered in the mesquite, calling softly.

Eventually Charlie took a deep, contented breath and said, 'You reckon Arkle's goin' after the Concho Flats bank?'

'Convinced of it,' Lane said. 'Rustlers steal cows. Bank robbers rob banks. Once you've cottoned on to how easy the one is, you don't pack it in and take up the hard work.'

'That being true makes it all the more important we get Arkle tonight,' Charlie Rivers said. 'But there ain't no easy way of prising a man out of a place he don't want to be prised out of.'

'No,' Lane agreed. 'But most line cabins are pretty much alike. One window, one door. If we can't get Arkle out, he sure ain't going nowhere while we're outside.'

After a while Charlie Rivers turned in his saddle and looked back the way they'd come.

'Hear something?'

'Maybe.' He faced front, cleared his throat. 'Maybe not. Probably Lije Coombs atop that awful black hearse, rattlin' after us like one of them harbingers of doom.'

'You've been drinking out of that silver flask of his,' Lane said, and Rivers flashed a grin as he pointed ahead.

The last of the sun was now no more than a pink glow on the underside of western cloud banks far away to their left. Its receding light was over-whelmed by a vast blackness across which stars were being sown like countless glistening seed pearls, and that night's moon was a wan disc floating low in the sky, promising brilliance.

Suddenly its pale light was reflected from the flat surface of slow-moving water. They rode down a gentle slope where willow branches were shifting silhouettes rattling in the strengthening breeze, and splashed quickly and easily through a wide, shallow ford that was never more than hock-deep.

As their mounts lunged up the far bank, Rivers called across, 'Buffalo Ridge, Rocky,' and Lane looked ahead to a line of hills that loomed as a low smudge against the luminescent night skies.

'Fifteen minutes ride,' he said, moving alongside Charlie Rivers. Again he caught the flash of pale skin as the other ranger turned his head to look over his shoulder, and for an instant felt a twinge of unease. Then, trusting his companion, knowing Rivers would holler fast enough if he was sure something was amiss, Lane turned his attention to the task ahead.

'This ain't no time for complicated tactics,' he said. 'I guess we've been in similar situations enough times before.'

'Sure,' Charlie Rivers agreed. 'Get under cover. Throw down on the cabin. Holler a warning, then set back and await developments.'

'Couldn't put it better,' Lane said with a slow smile.

With the river behind them and the rising moon revealing details of an eerie landscape of light and shade they put their horses to a fast lope across a level plain where the lush grass appeared to move before the breeze like the swell of a vast, inland ocean.

They traversed that swiftly, came upon a wide cattle trail which they crossed at an angle with a low rumble of hooves and a flurry of dust, rode a long sweep around a stand of trees where the shadows were deep and cold and made their way through a shallow, dry wash with the flinty sound of their passing throwing hollow echoes in their ears.

They emerged into an awesome silence and rode on. And all the time the dark mass of Buffalo Ridge loomed closer before the rising moon until, where the lushness of the plains gave way to coarse grass indicating the presence of bedrock, and terrain sparsely covered with rough scrub sloped gently up towards a ridge covered thickly by trees like a dark, heavy pelt, Rockwell Lane called a halt.

'I smell cattle,' he said quietly, and as he spoke they both heard the mournful bellow of a restless steer and knew that beyond the ridge slept Sam Wallace's longhorn herd.

Charlie Rivers sniffed the air and said drily, 'And I smell trouble. If that cabin's tucked away in the trees the moon's in the wrong place.'

'No trouble.' Lane said. 'We ride around the west slope, follow the deep shadow up along the edge of the trees.'

Rivers nodded, his eyes intent, and said softly, 'I've got them!' He raised an arm to point high and to the right, where a square of yellow light glimmered.

'Let's go.'

They rode the long way around the west end of the ridge, brushing through the richer grass before putting their eager horses to the scrub slope where the first dark trees covered what might have been the rump of a sleeping buffalo. Along those woods they rode through crackling deadfalls, their hats brushed by trailing branches, climbing at first then levelling off so that they rode easily around the wide curve of the tree line.

'Must be close,' Lane murmured, and at his indication they moved out, still in deep shadow but now clear of the deadfalls, hooves muffled.

'Woodsmoke,' Charlie Rivers said suddenly.

They drew rein up against a wooded spur, slid down into damp grass and quickly tethered their horses under the trees. Leather whispered as Winchesters were slid from scabbards. Cold metal glinted, then became dulled as they left their mounts and entered the blackness and with some difficulty fumbled their way through the timber of the spur to emerge in cold moonlight on the edge of a gradual slope.

The cabin was tucked in their trees to the left of the clearing, easily located by its lighted window but otherwise completely blanketed in shadow cast by the backdrop of thick timber. Smoke from the stove was plucked upward by the slight breeze to be snagged in the trees' branches and drift into the high moonlight like white mist. A voice carried to them. They clearly heard the clatter of a tin plate, another voice raised in anger.

'Here's as good as anywhere,' Rockwell Lane said, employing oft used words to make light of a tense situation. 'Now's as good as later.'

He dropped to one knee behind a thick pine and rested the rifle butt on a bed of needles, while Charlie Rivers moved some dozen paces to his right and settled down, Spencer at the aim. Then Lane lifted his cupped hand to his mouth.

'You there, in the cabin!' he roared.

The words rolled down the slope, were picked up

by the breeze and became lost. Almost at once, there was an almighty crash in the cabin and the yellow light winked out.

'Texas Rangers!' Lane yelled. 'Put down your weapons, come out with your hands high!'

The reply was a bellow of rage.

'Come and get us, Rangers!'

Rockwell Lane lifted his hand, brought it down. Away to his right Charlie Rivers's rifle cracked, the muzzle belching flame. They both heard the whirr of the slug before it slammed into the cabin's door. Then came the sound of shattering glass.

'Return fire,' Lane warned, and ducked down, as from the darkened window fire flared and a long gun blasted three times in rapid succession. The slugs snicked harmlessly through the trees, low and to the left.

'Hold your fire, Charlie.'

Lane came up off his knees and moved to join Rivers.

'My eyes're gettin' accustomed,' Charlie Rivers said, and spat in the grass. 'There's three horses in that corral. We guessed wrong.'

'Yeah, but their riders don't know where we are,' Lane said confidently, 'so we let 'em stew. They feel like talking, let 'em talk. They want to waste a few shells – let 'em. While they're settin' there sweatin', make your way round back of the cabin, come down—'

He got no further.

The door of the cabin slammed open. In the

instant of shocked silence three indistinct figures charged out and moved rapidly apart like flitting shadows. One shadow drifted into open moonlight. Charlie Rivers loosed one rapid shot, cursed as the shadow merged with the timber and was gone. Then from three different directions six-guns opened up. A hail of lead tore across the clearing in a deadly rain of accurate converging fire. A bullet tugged at Rivers's sleeve, dislodged his hat. Another seared the lobe of Lane's ear like the light touch of a red hot knife blade, and he felt warm blood trickle down his neck.

'Fall back!' Rockwell Lane shouted.

They stumbled into the trees, blindly retracing their steps as the firing stuttered to a halt. Their ears sang in the silence. Within seconds they were through the timber. They emerged into bright moonlight on the far side of the spur. One of their horses nickered a welcome as they approached.

And from somewhere not too far away, it was answered by an excited whinny.

'Cow hands,' Lane panted as he investigated his wound then put a bloody hand on the saddle horn and rammed home his rifle. 'Blue was wrong, they heard the gunfire, they're coming fast.'

'Too fast,' Rivers countered. 'Hell, the shootin's only just started, ain't been time for cow hands to get from the valley to here.' He swung into the saddle, pointed down the smooth line of trees curving along the swell of Buffalo Ridge, the line they had so recently followed.

Two riders could be seen some three quarters of a mile away, approaching fast, boldly urging their horses hard along the open, moonlit slope, cutting off any hope of escape in that direction.

'So that's what you were listening to back at the Concho,' Lane said.

'Wasn't sure,' Rivers said apologetically.

'I thought the fellers that killed Wilson had left town,' Lane said, warily eyeing the two horsemen. 'Well, that makes three times I've been wrong, so I guess it's your turn to talk tactics, Charlie.'

He listened to distant shouting, guessed that Arkle and his cronies had regrouped and were saddling up. That put three men to the north on fresh horses, two coming fast from the south. A barrier of thick timber cloaked the hillside above them. The way down was wide open, but . . .

As if reading his mind Charlie Rivers said, 'Three horses're rested. In open country, we're dead. Only way is through the woods, Rocky.'

At once they turned their mounts to the slope and moved swiftly from bright moonlight to dappled gloom and then the cushioned darkness under thick pines. They made twenty yards in haste, another twenty and were slowed to a stumbling walk as the slope steepened and became uneven, and the carpet of pine needles began to slide treacherously under the horses' hooves.

Bridles jingled. Saddles creaked. Both horses were blowing, their heads tossing, eyes rolling. A branch cracked like a pistol shot and Rivers cursed roundly as another snapped back, raking his cheek.

'Hell, they're into the woods both sides of us,' Lane warned, twisting in the saddle, peering anxiously into the darkness all around.

'Yeah,' Rivers said. 'And there's most likely more jayhawkers down there with the herd, which means we're heading—'

His words were chopped off as another branch snapped, leaving a jagged stump. His horse squealed in pain. Immediately a six-gun blasted, from out on the right but level with them. The slug ripped through the branches, showering them with twigs. Then a fierce volley of shots came from two different points to their left. Bullets slammed into pine trunks. Others hummed past like angry hornets.

'Goddammit, hold your fire!' a voice roared, and Charlie Rivers chuckled.

'Caught in their own crossfire,' he said joyfully. 'We lie down they'll end up plugging each other!'

Then, above them, they heard the crackle of timber. Through the thick woods higher up the hill dappled moonlight glinted on metal.

'One or more of 'em's worked round,' Lane gritted, and at once flattened himself along the dun's neck as the jayhawker up the slope opened up with a rifle.

'Return their fire?'

'No!'

'Then there's only one way to go, Rocky!'

'Back – and split up,' Lane acknowledged.

The crash of heavy bodies in the timber on both sides told him gunmen were closing in fast as he hauled on the reins to turn his horse, almost dragging it off its feet with his efforts then prudently letting it find its own footing on the shifting pine needles as it snorted and started down slope.

Close by, Charlie Rivers was also having trouble manoeuvring in the tight space. His quit a stirrup and lifted his leg high as his horse lurched heavily against a tree, half fell sideways out of the saddle and snatched desperately at a hanging branch.

He was swinging back into the saddle when again the uphill rifle blasted. Rockwell Lane clearly heard the sickening thump as the bullet smacked home into human flesh. It was followed by Charlie Rivers's strangled grunt. Lane turned to look back up the slope. He saw the shadowy figure bowed in the saddle, heard his partner moan, 'Ride, Rockwell, ride, I'm okay!', and clenching his teeth he strained forwards, flicked loose reins and urged the dun into a jinking run down through the trees.

Horse and rider exploded into the open, under clear night skies. They raced along the edge of the spur of timber and out onto clear ground. One man had been left on the cabin side of the wooded spur for such an eventuality. He leaped into the open, managed a single snap shot with a rifle that winged wide, then roared out a warning to Arkle and the other renegades.

Then the dun's flying hooves had carried Rockwell Lane over a grassy hump sparkling with dew to race headlong down a steep slope that gradually levelled out until there was nothing before them but the wide expanse of moonlit plain stretching ahead to the fork of the Conchos at San Angelo. The breeze was refreshingly cool on his face. The fading crackle of pistol fire was a reminder of a brush with death that maybe wasn't yet over.

But what of Charlie Rivers?

Lane had ridden fast for a considerable distance without thought for direction, when the realization that there was no pursuit brought him to his senses. He narrowed his eyes then, saw ahead of him the bleached out walls of the dry wash they had negotiated and beyond that the dark outline of trees, and knew that the dun had carried him back almost to the shallow ford a mile from Concho Flats.

In the brilliant moonlight, on the edge of the draw, Rockwell Lane paused in the saddle to build himself a smoke.

His first instinct was to continue on into town. There had been other times over the years when he and Charlie Rivers had, during the course of their many encounters with outlaws, been forced to head in different directions. Often, they had both been in deadly danger, but the simple ploy of forcing their adversaries to choose between one or the other of them – or divide their own forces – had always been successful.

But engraved on Rockwell Lane's mind was the sound of a bullet hitting flesh and muscle and the picture of Charlie Rivers slumped in his saddle as he rode away from dark woods riven by gunfire – and saved his own skin.

As he trickled smoke and listened to the soft blow of the dun's patient breathing, those images troubled Lane. And so after a further minute's deliberation he sighed, killed the cigarette and murmured softly to the dozing horse.

Then he turned his back on Concho Flats and set out to find the wounded Charlie Rivers.

Lane had no fears of again encountering Jake Arkle and the renegades. The rangers had gone hunting Arkle; Arkle was concerned with lining his pockets and staying out of jail. So he would have watched with a lot of satisfaction as both rangers hightailed away from the cabin at Buffalo Ridge.

In the moonlight the ridge was a dark, sleeping giant, the wide plain spread out before Lane like an open map. He rode back over much of the same route they had taken, but instead of turning to climb the west slope he rode east in the lee of the ridge to the point where the dun had carried him down from the upper slopes.

Here he paused. The moon had climbed high above the ridge's timber crest, and in the silvery, dew-soaked grass of the plain he clearly saw his own dark trail. Diverging from it were the tracks of another horse that had veered sharply after its headlong downward plunge. Those tracks led east, and as Lane lifted his head to follow that arrow-straight trail, his jaw tightened.

In that direction lay the fork of the Conchos –
and Sam Wallace's Running Irons ranch.

NINE

Seen from a distance, it might have been a redskin, and on a night such as this would have evoked an instant chill of fear.

At the ragged end of the trees, on the crest of a low rise, the pony and rider Lane had been seeking were stock-still, both fixed in that languid yet majestic attitude that has come to epitomize the eternal patience and watchfulness of the Plains Indian.

A flat high cloud floated across the bright face of the moon as the dun cantered easily up the slope and Rockwell Lane saw, in the shallow valley beyond the motionless blue roan and its rider, the sprawling buildings of a big ranch. The windows of the ranch house and the long bunkhouse were in darkness. The vanes of a windmill creaked distantly in the light breeze.

Maybe nine o'clock, Lane judged. Occupants of the bunkhouse in their blankets early. Well, with little to keep them entertained, they would be. Didn't *appear* to be a light at the house, but he couldn't see around the back. . . .

A long, moon-cast shadow slid down the hill and across the yard, and as one of the corralled horses nickered uneasily Lane rode alongside Charlie Rivers.

'Charlie?'

The reply was a grunt, a vague lift of the slumped shoulders, a sharp groan suppressed to a whimper as the movement caused pain.

The back of Rivers's coat was soaked with blood. His hands were clasped on the saddle horn, gloves stretched tight over the straining knuckles. He was hanging on by will power. Well, will power would keep him in the saddle, Rockwell Lane acknowledged – but it wouldn't keep him alive.

'Easy, feller, I'm takin' you down.'

He gathered in the motionless horse's reins, said, 'Hold on tight, Charlie,' and with infinite care set off to lead the injured ranger into the Running Irons.

The way down was across short, crisp grass. Harness jingled. A stone was dislodged with a faint rattle. The dun snorted, and Lane reached down, patted the damp neck. Then they were onto the hard-packed earth of the yard, and as hooves clattered there was movement in the corral behind the barn, and again a horse whickered, eagerly now.

'Quiet, damn you!' Lane swore, and with the cloud still shrouding the moon he eased the horses down the yard's gentle slope and in the deep shadows in front of the high timber barn he drew rein.

Their rough calculations had come up with eight

jayhawkers, including Arkle. Three at the Buffalo Ridge cabin left a possible five asleep in the Running Irons bunkhouse. Of those five, three had seen the two rangers together – and they would have shared their knowledge.

Taking Charlie Rivers into the bunkhouse was unlikely to be good for his health.

But once again there were a whole heap of ifs and maybes involved, and at that thought Lane glanced across at his semi-conscious partner with a faint smile, remembering with nostalgia their recent conversations.

One way or another, Jake Arkle must have heard about the two strangers in Concho Flats. But – although Lane didn't believe it – there was always the possibility he hadn't made the connection with the two rangers up in Santa Fe. Even if he had, Lane told himself, before the gunfight at Buffalo Ridge it could only have been a suspicion – so maybe Arkle had been keeping his mouth shut until absolutely certain.

He'd be certain now; they'd declared their presence, and their intention; but the cabin was ten miles away, in which case . . .

Judas Priest, what the hell am I doing arguing with myself? Rockwell Lane thought angrily. Here's Charlie hanging onto life by a thread and I'm sitting in the middle of a yard playing mind games with—

The sound of a gun cocking damn near made him wet his pants.

A shadow moved over on the house's long gallery.

A quiet, gravelly voice said, 'Leave your pard where he is, get down off your horse and walk over here with your hands high.'

'What I'd rather do,' Lane said, 'is lead his horse over there so you and me can get him inside the house.'

'You think you've got a choice?'

'I've got a duty to do what I can to save his life. Right now that's the best idea I can come up with.'

Seconds passed in silence. The cloud slid away from the moon and as the shadows fled Rockwell Lane saw a tall, rawboned man with iron-grey hair standing at the back of the gallery to one side of the open door. A rifle was cradled easily in the crook of his left arm. His eyes glinted like hard steel.

Sam Wallace, he guessed.

Then Charlie Rivers moaned.

'Bring him across,' Wallace said, and he bent down and stood the rifle against the wall.

Lane swung down from the saddle, left the dun in the shadows by the barn and led Charlie's horse across the moonlit yard to the house. By the time he reached it Wallace was down off the gallery, and together they eased Rivers down off his horse and struggled with his dead weight up the steps and into the living room.

As they lay the wounded ranger down on the settee Wallace said gruffly, 'Last time he was in this room, my daughter was lying there.'

Lane let that one go, went back to close the front door – and in doing so shut out Sam Wallace's rifle.

A match scraped behind him. There was the faint smell of coal oil as a lamp wick caught and the room was bathed in yellow light.

'Never did give me his name,' Wallace said.

'Charlie Rivers,' Lane said. 'He needs a doc.'

Wallace grunted. 'You had one idea, I've got another. The kitchen's out back, hot water on the stove, a bowl and cloths handy. If I can't fix him, he's as good as dead.'

For a moment Rockwell Lane hesitated. Then, as Sam Wallace glared at him and began rolling up his sleeves, he took a quick look at Charlie Rivers's chalk-white face and headed for the kitchen.

The match flared, lighting the rugged planes of Sam Wallace's face and shining in the hard grey eyes as he brought the flame close and applied it to the tip of his cigar.

And, watching him, Rockwell Lane knew he had seen that face somewhere before.

Not on Wanted dodgers. Hell, no, this man would surely warrant more auspicious publicity. But he'd seen him, and not in the flesh – because if he had, he'd know for sure where, and when.

Charlie Rivers was still, his breathing deep and regular. His eyelids were closed to narrow slits and, whether in the drifting watchfulness of semi-consciousness or the blindness of deep coma, the eyes within shone out wetly in the lamplight. Somewhere halfway between the two, Lane thought, noting the hands thrust beneath the faded Navajo blanket that covered the ranger from ankles to waist. Bandages swathed his torso, already stained with fresh blood. The naked skin of his shoulders glistened in the lamplight.

'He gets over the shock, he'll pull through,' Wallace said, blowing a cloud of smoke towards the low rafters and squinting across at Lane. He was relaxed in one of the comfortable chairs, grey hair damp, long legs stretched out, his shirt sleeves rolled back to below the elbow. 'But, tell the truth,' he added, 'it ain't him concerns me.'

Rockwell Lane sat opposite him, in the chair he'd dropped into when the worst of the crude operation was over and Wallace, hands bloody, face streaming with sweat, had told him roughly he could be of no more use. Immeasurably relieved, his mind deliberately closed to the low moans of his partner, Lane had sat smoking as Wallace probed for the bullet embedded in Rivers's knotted shoulder muscles; had felt his own muscles relax as the misshapen hunk of lead rattled into the tin bowl.

Lane had deliberately chosen a chair that gave him a clear view of both door and window. While blocking out the sounds of Charlie Rivers's torment, his eyes and ears had been alert for any signs of awakening life from the bunkhouse. He had heard nothing; in the bright moonlight, nothing had moved. Yet his vigilance had never relaxed, his hand never straying far from the holstered Colt he had shifted around to the front of his thigh.

'No,' Lane admitted now, 'Charlie can't cause you much trouble.'

Wallace chuckled. 'Nor you, my friend. That's not what I meant. What concerns me is what to do with you now.'

'Charlie'll sleep the clock around.' Lane forced a careless shrug. 'Best thing is for me to head back to Concho Flats, bring the doc out first thing.'

'No.' Wallace shook his head. 'I told your pard I couldn't take a chance. That still holds, particularly now the suspicions I've had about you two are firming up some.'

'What the hell is going on around here, Wallace?' Rockwell Lane said quietly.

'Mister, I'm aiming to sell some beef. That's all you need to know.'

Lane smiled faintly. 'Jake Arkle being around suggests there's more to it.'

'That name keeps cropping up,' Wallace said tersely. 'First your friend, now you. That's uncommon interest you're showing.' He looked pensively at the thread of smoke curling from his cigar, then shook his head firmly. 'Jake Arkle and his men,' Wallace said deliberately, 'are part of the crew driving that herd north—'

'Last I heard of him he was on the run, in Santa Fe,' Rockwell Lane cut in. 'Who brought him here?'

'I did.'

The new voice came from behind Lane. He turned quickly in the deep chair, his hand instinctively reaching for his Colt. But the dark-haired man standing in the doorway at the back of the room had his six-gun out and levelled, and Lane cursed mentally as he let his hand fall away from his holster.

'Well now,' Wallace said harshly. 'So you've finally decided to come clean.'

'Who are these men, pa?'

'Their names don't matter. Seeing as we want the same thing, though for different reasons, they're trouble for both of us.' Wallace pushed himself up from the chair, stuck the cigar in the corner of his mouth and said angrily, 'Take him across to the bunkhouse, Vern. Wake that man Phillips. Tell him I want this man held.'

'I guess you do, don't you?' The young man's voice was mocking, the bruises on his face livid as he moved into the lamplight. 'Be a cruel shame to throw away all those years, all that running and hiding, for the sake of a few thousand hea—'

'Do it!'

Wallace's grey eyes flashed fire. His big fists were clenched at his side, his jaw muscles bulging. The boy grinned. Then he gestured at Rockwell Lane with the Colt, and when the ranger came up out of the chair he stepped close and deftly plucked the Colt from its holster.

'Now move.'

The dark eyes met Lane's, held his gaze, then slid away. The ranger walked to the door, opened it and stepped out onto the gallery.

As he paused in the cold light and took a deep breath of clear air, he swiftly estimated his chances.

Charlie was always quoting odds. Well, now was probably the best time to make his move. But Vern Wallace's shifty eyes suggested he was unstable, liable to blast away if startled – and the gun in his hand was cocked.

That gun was suddenly rammed painfully hard into his spine.

Chance gone. Ruefully, Lane went down the steps, past Rivers's dozing horse, and started across the yard. He heard boots on timber and a cough behind him, knew Sam Wallace had come out to keep a watchful eye on his son, would probably pick up the rifle.

'This don't make sense,' Lane said softly, half turning his head. 'I don't know what the hell goes on but this way ain't the answer.'

'What goes on,' Vern Wallace said, 'is the old man gets his comeuppance.'

Lane's horse nickered from the shadows by the barn. Dust scraped under his boots as they neared the bunkhouse. The ranger couldn't believe what he was hearing.

'You get back at your old man through these jayhawkers? You're out of your mind.'

'No. Two thousand head're worth a hundred thousand bucks in Kansas.' Suddenly there was pride in the voice. 'My cut's a third. I ride as Jake Arkle's *segundo*.'

'The hell you do! Listen, kid—'

'Cut out that goddamn talking!' Sam Wallace's roar echoed across the yard.

And then they were at the bunkhouse door.

Still glowering, Sam Wallace went into the house, shut the door and turned, rifle slack in his hand.

'Stay right there,' Charlie Rivers said huskily. 'I reckon I can hold this pistol for maybe half a minute – so just remember the last thing I'll keep a hold of is the trigger.'

'This won't get you anywhere,' Sam Wallace said, steely eyes already darting, assessing his chances. He looked at the unsteady, white-knuckled hand, the eyes glazed with pain. . . .

He took a step forward.

'Don't!' The pistol jerked. Wallace froze in mid-stride, eased his foot down. Lying propped against the end of the settee, Rivers grinned crookedly, the cold sweat streaming down his face. 'What this gets is time,' he said tightly, 'for Rockwell Lane.'

Wallace shook his head. 'The only place Lane's going is inside the bunkhouse at the wrong end of my son's hogleg,' he said with a bitter smile.

'You believe that,' Charlie Rivers said, 'and you ain't never come across Rockwell Lane when his dander's up.' He watched with satisfaction as Sam Wallace's angular frame jerked with shock and the smile became a grimace of disbelief as, from the direction of that bunkhouse, a six-gun blasted.

Again the six-gun ground into Lane's spine. Vern Wallace reached past him, unlatched the door and pushed it open. The gun was removed, a boot took its place, and Lane tripped over the step as he was catapulted into darkness.

He came up hard against a table, cracked his shin on a bench, caught hold of an upright to steady himself and heard a tin cup hit the floor and roll. Moonlight flooded in through the open door. Across the room a man tumbled, cursing, out of bed in his underwear. Another crashed to the floor still in his blankets. A gun was cocked, and Lane ducked back as a wild shot blasted and a slug whanged off the door frame.

'Cut it out, Tag!'

Vern Wallace yelled in a high, scared voice. The man called Tag growled, 'What the hell goes on?' Then someone padded across the floor towards the table. A match flared, scorched careless fingers, drew a coarse stream of profanity from its wielder and blinked out.

Now!

Rockwell Lane dropped into a fast crouch. He kicked his right leg out straight, swept it around and slammed his bent left elbow backwards into Vern Wallace's soft underbelly. His ankles hooked by the sweeping foot, the man by the table crashed to the floor. Behind Lane, the rancher's son gasped explosively, grabbed his guts and folded like a wet cloth. Still down on his heels, Lane reached up and grabbed two fistfuls of shirt. Then he straightened his legs. He drove up hard from the floor and hurled the sagging youngster bodily at the renegades.

Wallace's flying body hit the man called Tag. The two men tumbled backwards onto the bed. One leg splintered, tipping them onto the floor. A flailing arm hit the wall and again the six-gun blasted. A bullet drove harmlessly through the roof.

Rockwell Lane was only vaguely aware of this pandemonium. After releasing Vern Wallace he took two fast strides towards the open door and flung himself through the opening as, from the far side of the bunkhouse, another six-gun opened up and a slug whistled over his head.

Then he was outside and sprinting across the yard towards the barn just as the moon slid behind a cloud and blanketed the ranch premises in darkness.

But – where was Sam Wallace? He'd exploded out of the bunkhouse into bright moonlight, so why no rifle fire from the gallery of the big house?

The bunkhouse now sounded like a border saloon on a Saturday night. Men were yelling in anger, blundering about in total confusion. His boots slapping the dust, Lane heard an almighty clang behind him as the stove was knocked over. The iron chimney was dragged downwards, ripping away roof shingles. Two men hit the doorway running. More curses rang out over the yard as they kicked and elbowed their way free.

Then Lane reached his waiting dun. Two six-guns began blazing. Bullets punched holes in the barn's doors above his head. He flung himself into the saddle, scooped up the reins, spun the horse and

applied the spurs. In one powerful bound the eager
gelding was at full gallop. In a night of luminous
shadows it streaked down the side of the barn,
brushed along the slick poles of the corral, leaped
over a clutter of logs and boxes and hammered past
an outlying open shed. Seconds later it was pounding across open countryside, carrying Rockwell
Lane away from the Running Irons.

Behind him in the darkness howls of frustration
rent the air. Six-guns crackled, a voice roared, someone yelled faintly, 'He'll be heading for town, go get
the . . .'

Then the carefree breeze had borne the words
skywards, and all that mattered to Lane was the wind
in his face, the taste of dust on his lips and the
comforting beat of his horse's hooves and, as the
moon sailed into open skies and the way became
clear, he stretched out along his mount's neck and
settled down to a long, fast ride to save his life.

In the event, it didn't turn out that way. Over the
next mile he glanced back several times. Eventually,
convinced that the renegades had not set off in
pursuit, he sat up, eased the dun back to an easy trot
and set his thoughts to the task ahead.

Whoever had shouted had been wrong on one
count: he was not heading for town. The innate
caution that was an essential part of Lane's charac-
ter was more than offset by a stubborn refusal to
take things lying down. Knock him over, he'd
bounce back up. Turn him in one direction, he'd go
the other. Best him in a fight – well, you might win

a battle but you never did best Rockwell Lane in a war, for the reasons already mentioned and a few, like the legendary Texas ranger badge, that he preferred to keep as hole cards.

So Captain Rockwell Lane of the Texas Rangers cut across country from the Running Irons with anger smouldering inside him, a thin smile playing across his dark features – and a conviction that the course most likely to bring him success was to pretend the earlier gun battle at the cabin never happened.

Hell, why not? Already the idea of a second surprise attack was taking shape in his mind, and as his optimistic mood transmitted itself to the dun the animal's step became light and springy, and as its head lifted its nostrils flared eagerly towards the dark smudge of hills that was already visible some distance ahead.

Lane had an idea what he was doing was on the wild side even for an incautious man – which, of course, he was not – so as he rode west towards the ridge he did his best to devise a foolproof plan that would see Jake Arkle caught like a rabbit in a trap.

The best idea he could come up with was to sneak up behind the cabin, start a fire going against the back wall or maybe on the roof, then wait up on the hillside and shoot the bandits as they ran out of the burning building.

All that fanciful notion made him do was throw back his head and laugh at the moon, and as the gelding turned its head to roll his eye inquisitively at

him Lane leaned over, cuffed the horse affection-
ately around the head and gave up.

'Hell, horse,' he said wryly, 'who'm I supposed to
be fooling? The only reason I'm headin' back to
Buffalo Ridge is because I turned you the wrong
darned way out of the Running Irons – and the only
six-shooter I had's stuck down the front of Vern
Wallace's pants!'

With a shake of his head he dragged out the
makings and, settling his body to the horse's gait,
began rolling a smoke.

By the time the cigarette had been smoked from
end to end in a leisurely way and flicked away into
the night-wet mesquite, the ridge loomed large
above him and Lane knew that, accidental or not,
he was heading for a show-down of his own making.

Fancy schemes were out. If he and Rivers had
stayed mounted, kept their eyes on the front of the
cabin instead of trying to watch every which way at
the same time, they would've got Arkle at the first
attempt. Lane wouldn't make that mistake again.
One shouted warning, then any man stepping out
the door with a gun in his fist would be met by a hail
of lead.

This time, too, he forsook the approach across
the long slope from the west. He'd already proved
back at the Running Irons that men tangled in blankets groping their way up out of the fog of sleep
were at a disadvantage. If the bandits' horses in the
corral were going to hear or scent his approach, give
the alarm and take away the advantage of surprise,

the best thing to do was to go in the short way, fast and hard.

Spread before him as he approached the steep slope, the criss-crossing tracks were still visible in the dew-soaked grass below the ridge. His own dun's, and those of Charlie Rivers's sorrel. Nobody else had ridden this way down from the ridge.

Rockwell Lane reached down to his saddle boot, slid out his Winchester, lifted it and jacked a shell into the breech. Then, with a final squint up to the high fringe of dark pines outlined against clear skies adrift with pink skeins of thin cloud, he took a deep breath and set the dun at the slope.

Lane went up the side of the hill sitting loose in the saddle, riding with his knees, both hands holding the Winchester high. He let the dun step and lunge over ridges and mounds, half listening as loose rocks rattled from beneath the thrusting hooves, most of his attention tuned to the slopes above where the line cabin nestled in the small clearing cut into the first line of thick trees.

Long before he reached that point the brooding mass of Buffalo Ridge had smothered the light, and they moved through damp shadow where the first white mists of a distant dawn were gathering in hollows and spreading their chill.

Then he was over the last hump, had crested the grassy rise that brought him to the spur of trees on the edge of the clearing. And there he touched the reins, paused.

The dun snorted, breath whistling through flared

nostrils. Rockwell Lane settled his rifle and kneed the horse around so they were side on to the dark cabin; let his eyes range over the crude board gallery, the unlighted window, then drift to the corral, waiting patiently for night vision to come so that he could probe the gloom.

Nothing moved.

Lane eased his weight in the saddle, edged the dun along the trees, listened to hooves sucking in wet mud as the horse traversed a weed-choked fold where water trickled. . . .

The corral was empty.

With a muttered curse Lane kneed the dun down the gentle slope from the trees and across the expanse of grass to the cabin. He swung down alongside the gallery, left the reins trailing, stomped up onto the loose boards half hoping that Jake Arkle would come bursting out through the door with guns blazing – but knowing that wasn't going to happen.

Rockwell Lane lifted a boot and kicked the cabin door open with the bitter realization that the jayhawkers had gone. When he went inside he was met by emptiness; only the warmth and stink of their recent presence remained to mock him. . . .

TEN

The corroded hinges groaned, then squealed in protest as the massive door was scraped open across the hard dirt floor under pressure from Zac Slaughter's thrusting shoulder.

Cold moonlight flooded in. Draught hit the fire of stunted mesquite branches that crackled and spat in the huge stone fireplace. A blackened pot hung swaying over the blazing logs. Sparks flew madly up the wide chimney, and the light from the dancing flames sent shadows leaping and cavorting across the crumbling bare walls.

'Leave it open,' Jake Arkle growled.

He was stretched out on spread blankets in front of the fire, dark head on his sweat blackened saddle, gunbelt by his side next to the Winchester in its unbuckled saddle scabbard. Blade Quatro was sitting up against the wall next to the fire, fancy vest glistening, a black cheroot smouldering between the fingers of one hand, while with the others he picked absently at his bandages.

Slaughter kicked the heavy oak door, glared at

Arkle, and said, 'Can't close the goddamn thing anyway.' He came on into the room, carrying with him the smell of horses and cold night, hitching up his gunbelt and glowering across at Blade Quatro.

'If a man ain't fit enough to tend to his own animals, what the hell use is he likely to be when we ride into Concho Flats?' he demanded.

'Quatro ain't ridin' with us,' Arkle said, and his black eyes glittered as Slaughter first gaped in disbelief, then scowled as anger took hold. 'You want a cripple slowin' you down inside the bank?' Arkle asked, and from alongside the fire Quatro hissed angrily.

'Who the hell're you callin' a cripple?' he snapped.

'The only man in the room with a bullet hole in his leg,' Arkle replied, and laughed softly. 'Cool down, both of you. It was Zac's idea to get us spare mounts from the roundup camp, Blade's to bring them here to the Mission San Luis 'stead of wastin' time hangin' around out at the line cabin. Now it's my turn. And what I say is, me and Zac do the bank, Blade stays here with the spare mounts.'

'And I say we draw straws for it.'

'Say what the hell you like, Zac,' Arkle said, and uncoiled lithely from the blankets to come up on his feet and head for the door.

He stepped into the opening, a tall, bewhiskered figure radiating strength, and looked off beyond the line of picketed horses and over the flat plain where the grass whispered in the breeze towards the dark, silhouetted shapes that were the buildings of Concho Flats in the far distance, the sprinkling of yellow lights.

'Only fair way, Jake,' Zac Slaughter grumbled insistently at his shoulder. 'Short straw stays behind.'

'See it?' Jake Arkle said softly. 'Over there, where those lights're scattered? That's my cash, settin' in Alan Moffatt's bank just a-waitin' for us to walk in, pick it up.'

'Sam Wallace's cash,' Slaughter said, and spat in the dust.

'No, Sam Wallace has had the loan of it, the use of it – but it never was his.'

'You listenin' to what I'm sayin'?' Slaughter growled, suddenly changing tack. 'Spare mounts can look after themselves. We need three guns. I say Blade Quatro's fit enough to walk into the bank.'

'Judas Priest!' Jake Arkle said, breath whistling through pinched nostrils. He swung around, placed his hand flat on the slab-muscled chest, thrust his face close to the lean gunman's and said fiercely, 'It ain't Blade's fault for gettin' shot, but the man can get in the way, Zac, ruin a simple bank robbery, get us all killed—'

A slim shadow bobbed close, brought with it the stink of a strong cheroot. Blade Quatro said, 'Zac's part right, Jake. Only there ain't no need for straws. We ride in together. Two of you work inside the bank. That leaves me outside, holding the horses, watching your backs.' Under the sweeping black moustache his teeth flashed white in the moonlight.

'If I'm going to be a horse minder, I'll feel better doing it close to the action.'

'On our own we're forced to tie the horses, and that wastes time, goin' in and comin' out,' Zac Slaughter said persuasively, and Jake Arkle let his breath go in an explosive gust of frustration.

'All right, goddammit! Maybe you're right.'

'Give me a Winchester and enough shells and I'll hold the town at bay,' Quatro said with joy in his voice, and Jake Arkle laughed.

'Get some sleep, both of you. Tomorrow you'll be rich men.'

ELEVEN

Yawning and scratching, Blue Hills climbed down the shaky ladder from the hay loft over his stable when the sun was flooding the square and painting the walls of Concho Flats's bank a brilliant gold.

He swilled his face at the pump out back, ran a testing hand over his whiskers and decided shaving could wait another couple of days. Then he turned his keen blue eyes to gaze north along the wide alley between decaying shacks that led to open country-side and, a mile out, the ford across the Concho.

Well, there sure was no damn sign of Rockwell Lane or his partner. That didn't guarantee Arkle and his crew had bested them, or even that they were in trouble, but it pointed that way – and the tall dark Texas Ranger's request had been clear enough.

If he hadn't showed up by dawn, go warn Alan Moffatt to expect trouble.

The little ostler built himself a smoke, wandered back up the runway and spent the next half hour tending to the horses in his care, by which time the sun was warning the town the day was going to be a

125

scorcher, and Blue Hills's belly was telling him never mind the weather, was his throat cut, or what?

The café was close to the bank. Alan Moffatt would be at least an hour before leaving his grand house to open up for business. There was still time for Lane and Rivers to ride in, but in any case breakfast seemed like a good idea. Hills unlocked the office, buckled on his gunbelt and set out across the wide square. On the way, for some reason, his eyes were drawn to a gap between the buildings he was approaching, through which he could see the hazy outlines of the derelict Mission San Luis.

Then he flicked away his cigarette, and with a final glance at the barred doors of Moffatt's bank he pushed on into the café to be greeted by a mighty sizzling and the mouthwatering aroma of frying beef.

Rockwell Lane awoke with a start that scared him half to death, set his heart thundering in his chest and almost tipped him sideways onto the cabin floor.

The broken back of the chair he'd slept in had pressed a painful, uneven groove across his spine. On the table's stained surface, under his gloved right hand, the Winchester pointed towards the closed door beneath which the icy draught of morning sighed and moaned. Under the table his stretched out legs pointed the same way, and inside his boots his feet were as stiff and as cold as the Winchester's blued barrel.

Hell, Lane thought, yawning cavernously, he was some goddamn ranger. Arkle and all seven of his jayhawkers could have ridden straight through the cabin door without bothering to open it, and plugged him while he sat there snoring!

Mentally cursing his stupidity, Lane came stiffly up out of the chair and hobbled and stamped about the cabin until the blood came unglued in his veins and some warmth and feeling reached his feet. Then he stretched up to the rafters until tight muscles crackled, dragged open the door and stepped out onto the dripping gallery.

The ride up had been steep, the cabin set high under the pine covered crest of Buffalo Ridge. The sun was already up over the eastern horizon, painting golden fingers across the high, flaring clouds and creating dazzling patterns on the dew-soaked grass of the clearing. But it was not yet hot enough to lift the white mists thinly blanketing the rolling plains, and though Lane knew where Concho Flats lay, the closest he could get to picking it out was the glittering, distant ribbon he knew was the Concho.

Where had Arkle and the jayhawkers gone when they left the cabin? If they had ridden for the Running Irons, he would certainly have blundered into them in the moonlight. That was out – so maybe they'd ridden the opposite way, straight over the ridge, reckoning that after the dust up with the rangers at the cabin it was safer to spend the night with the weary riders watching over the growing longhorn herd.

Wherever they'd melted away to in the moonlight hours of the night, Lane knew the sudden arrival of Texas Rangers on the scene would have altered the outlaws' plans in only one respect: they would now be consumed with urgency, desperate to finish what they'd set out to do, and flee for the border.

Which still left Rockwell Lane sitting on a mighty precarious fence. Common sense told him his best bet was to ride to Concho Flats and await developments. But he'd already spoken to Mick Reilly, and asked Blue Hills to warn Alan Moffatt. So he'd done pretty well all he could to prepare the town for a raid on its bank – and as a Texas Ranger his job was to go after outlaws, not sit and wait for them to ride in and surrender.

Lane jumped down into the wet grass, circled round behind the cabin and walked twenty yards into the woods to where he'd tethered his horse. He was greeted by a soft whicker. A warm muzzle was pressed against his neck and the horse blew gently. Smiling faintly, absently, Lane led the dun out of the woods, and once it was happily nosing at the hay in the corral he returned to the cabin.

Still worrying at the problem, his mind some ten miles away with Mick Reilly, Lije Coombs and Concho Flats's feisty little ostler, he located some dried-out jerky, gnawed off a hunk, then went outside, found the patch of soggy ground he'd ridden through and followed it up to the cold spring that bubbled from beneath a mossy rock.

A gulp of crystal-clear water washed down the salt

beef; two handfuls dashed in his face took away his
breath and cleared the remaining cobwebs. Lane
dried his face on his bandanna, hunkered down in
the sweet grass, reached to his shirt pocket for the
makings – and from behind the cabin the dun
whickered, and was immediately answered from
afar.

'Hell-fire!'

Lane swore, sprang to his feet and sprinted for
the corral. He lifted his saddle from the open
fronted lean-to, heaved it up and over the dun,
cinched up and within seconds had led the saddled
horse around into the clearing. There he clattered
into the cabin, planted his black hat on his head
and grabbed his Winchester. Outside again he
grasped the horn, stepped into the saddle, slid the
rifle into its boot and swung the dun into a
stretched-out lope down the wet grass slope.

Time . . . time . . . He had moved fast but it had
all taken time – and now, like the approach of ghost
riders, the steady beat of hooves came drifting up to
him out of the blanket of mist.

But where the sounds were coming from, it was
impossible to judge.

Then the dun had reached the mist, had plunged
into it to bear down swiftly on a narrow belt of trees
lining the lower slopes, had raced recklessly on
through those woods and down a steep bank and, as
the ground swiftly levelled and the drum of hooves
seemed to swell all around him, Lane reined back,
sent the horse lunging back up the bank and along

the edge of the trees then again pulled it to a halt and backed it out of sight under the dark, drooping branches.

He slid from the saddle. As the mists swirled and parted at the riders' approach he reached a hand up, felt the animal's tremor of excitement and lightly pinched the dun's nostrils.

Half a dozen horsemen emerged from the mist on cantering mounts. Ragged, unshaven men, heavily armed, wearing coarse woollen coats over cavalry trousers. Coming from the east: from the Running Irons. And as they rattled past, not ten feet away, their shaggy, Stetsoned heads bobbing level with Lane's boots, from the deep shelter of the trees he studied their set faces and saw none he recognized.

He cautiously watched them ride away in a westerly direction, thought he saw the slight swing in towards the slope as the cantering horsemen were again swallowed by the mist and hazarded a shrewd guess that they were heading around the western point of Buffalo Ridge, making for the roundup camp.

Did that mean the outlaw leader, Jake Arkle, was there, Lane wondered? Was he seeing the outlaw band assemble, witnessing the abandonment of the spurious trail drive, the start of the ride on Concho Flats that would end in the bloody raid on the bank?

Lane swung back into the saddle, eased out from under the trees, down the bank and across the crushed, trampled grass that, apart from the still-warm odour of their horses, was the only sign of the riders' passing.

Yes, he decided, it seemed likely.

It also put paid to any thoughts he might have had of leaving the town to fend for itself while he went gunning for Arkle. With all the outlaws assembled in one place it would be a hopeless act of bravado that would see him riding in alone to be met by a withering hail of hot lead – and far from being a bank raid by three tough renegades who might conceivably be repulsed by the tough little ostler and his determined friends, this looked certain to be a lightning raid by eight ruthless desperadoes who would ride into Concho Flats with blazing guns and sweep all before them.

That was one way it could end, Lane thought, his mind racing.

But . . . if he got there first, ordered the bank shut and barred . . . turned Concho Flats into a ghost town . . . transformed the well-planned bank raid into an abortive fiasco. . . .

His dark face set in a mask of grim determination, Rockwell Lane put spurs to the dun and headed for the Concho at a headlong gallop that he was convinced was a desperate race against time.

'You've got grease on your whiskers,' Alan Moffatt said, his mouth puckered with distaste.

'And you'll have egg all over your fat face if you don't listen to me,' Blue Hills snarled.

Moffatt poked in a finger to mark the papers he

was sorting, glanced sideways at Henry, a skinny clerk in a shiny black suit who was pretending not to listen, then leaned over the counter and said with deliberately offensive clarity, 'Sam Wallace organised a cattle drive up the Chisholm Trail to Kansas, to be carried out by Jake Arkle and his riders. The profits from the sale of those cattle will be deposited in this bank.' He smirked. 'Money is coming in, not going out.'

'You don't believe that any more than I do,' Hills scoffed angrily. 'You're siding with Sam Wallace, under the mistaken idea that giving those outlaws his cattle'll keep the bulk of his cash in your safe.'

Moffatt shrugged dismissively, licked a finger and flicked papers. 'Wallace's business deals are his affair. I own a bank.'

'Today. Tomorrow you'll own a bare room, and an empty safe.'

Blue Hills had both hands planted flat on the counter and was glaring furiously at Alan Moffatt through narrowed blue eyes. He had left the café with a full belly, spoken briefly to Lije Coombs who was polishing the big black hearse with rags borrowed from the gunsmith, waved to Mick Reilly as he emerged yawning from the Pleasure Palace with a mop and bucket, then stormed into the bank as soon as he heard the iron bolts slam back and the big doors open for business.

Without preamble he had informed Alan Moffatt that, according to two fine Texas Rangers who were even now out attempting to apprehend the felons, the bank was in danger of being robbed by a band of dangerous outlaws.

Moffatt had laughed in his face.

But Blue Hills's last words about an empty safe appeared to have hit home, and as he continued to sort through the sheaf of papers his eyes began to flick nervously towards the open door.

'Rockwell Lane said he'd be back by dawn,' Hills pressed on. 'He ain't, so now I've done what he asked and you've been warned.' He glared at the balding top of the bank owner's lowered head, curled a lip and said, 'A heap of them gold coins tucked away in that safe belong to me. If you need a guard for the day I can set in the shade on Mick Reilly's gallery, keep an eye on here and still watch the stable for customers. You hear me holler, shut and bolt the doors.' He looked past Moffat, asked, 'You got a back door?' and at the banker's quick nod said, 'When the doors are locked, you and Henry get out that way, fast.'

Moffatt carefully squared the papers and put them under the counter. The clerk came over, slid a paper in front of him. Moffatt signed it without bothering to look, then lifted his head to stare worriedly through the door and across the square.

'Sam should have anticipated something like this, warned me himself,' he said. He was talking to himself, and now there was a glint of annoyance in his eyes. 'Feller should have known Arkle wouldn't settle for anything less than his total ruin, not after what he . . .'

His voice trailed off, his mouth snapped shut.

'Sounds like Sam's over a barrel,' Blue Hills suggested.

'Yes, well . . .' Moffatt shrugged his heavy shoulders as if shaking off a mood of depression. A film of sweat had appeared on his white forehead. He cocked an eyebrow at Hills. 'If you're right. . . . If these men are, er, planning something – from which direction should we expect them?'

'Straight as an arrow from Buffalo Ridge,' Hills said flatly. 'Over the Concho, in back of the stable and across the square.'

'All right.' Moffatt nodded, then coughed delicately into the back of his hand. 'I'd, er, appreciate your help, Hills.'

Whistling through his teeth and rolling his eyes, the ostler swung on his heel and went out into the dust and the heat. He tramped the diagonal line across towards the Pleasure Palace, turned his head to watch Lije Coombs climb like a big black spider onto his seat, click his tongue and set the sleek chestnut horse high stepping across the square with the gleaming hearse in tow, cracked a brief smile at the dazzling sight then hopped up onto the gallery.

Mick Reilly sent a wave of sudsy water slopping across the boards, then called cheerfully, 'You convince that miserable bastard he needs protection?' He shook his head and turned to reach for his mop.

And all hell was let loose.

With a tremendous bang the huge, engraved side

window of the hearse disintegrated and a million shards of sparkling glass exploded into the air and rained down on the square. The chestnut horse bolted. Lije Coombs let loose with a demented, caterwauling howl of fury, hauled on the traces and leaped up to stand erect on the seat and wave a bony fist, beads of glass dripping from the brim of his hat.

Coombs was still squawking, trying to balance with braced legs on the bouncing seat and slow the careering hearse when three riders burst from the alley between the bank and the café.

'Jayhawkers!' Reilly roared, and the bucket went flying as he dived in through the saloon's swing doors.

Blue Hills's eyes gleamed. He slapped his holster, drew his Colt and stepped to the end of the gallery. As he did so two of the riders piled out of the saddle, hit the ground running and charged into the bank with drawn six-guns.

The third man, dark, with a flamboyant moustache and a bloodstained left leg, held the three horses' bunched reins in one hand and with the other swept the square with a still-smoking Winchester.

Blue Hills flattened himself against the saloon's wall. The rifle muzzle swung his way.

'Don't even think about it!' Blade Quatro roared.

And as the hearse was at last dragged to a creaking, shuddering halt, the sun-drenched square of Concho Flats became deathly still.

TWELVE

The gunfire was like the sharp crackle of a distant fire as Rockwell Lane sent the dun galloping across the ford in a shower of glittering spray that painted shimmering rainbows across the glassy waters of the Concho.

A mile!

He recalled Blue Hills's words, went over the previous night's ride, and his jaw muscles bunched as he leaned forward in the saddle and urged more speed from the racing horse.

Shiny gravel flew from beneath the flashing hooves as they thundered up the bank. They tore past the willows, the gallant dun stretched out across the flat grassland, and through eyes narrowed against the wind Lane watched the buildings of Concho Flats grow larger, recognized the yawning entrance to the wide alley between mouldering tar-paper shacks, beyond that the high outline of Blue Hills's livery stable.

Then, abruptly, he had reached the town.

He hammered down the alley, raced past the

corral and approached the livery stable at break-
neck speed. Somewhere not far away a rifle blasted.
Lead screamed through the air. A man roared, in
pain or fury. A six-gun cracked.

Lane rode headlong into the barn's dim runway,
dragged the sweating horse to a slithering halt on
loose straw, leaped from the saddle, flicked the reins
loosely around an upright and slid the Winchester
from its scabbard.

He went with caution towards the square, sidling
up to the barn's wide main doors, jacking a shell
into the rifle's breech as he went. He stared out
onto a vista of white dust and brown grass under
dazzling sunlight, his nostrils wrinkling to the harsh
tang of gunpowder, his narrowed eyes taking in a
situation that seemed to make the jayhawkers' position impregnable.

Mick Reilly was pinned down on the gallery of the
Pleasure Palace, on one knee, the shotgun that
made him a force to be reckoned with behind his
bar useless at this range, held impotently in both
ham-like hands.

Blue Hills was down behind the steps under the
hitch rail. He was less vulnerable than Reilly, but still
unable to threaten the bank raiders with his six-gun.
With a wide expanse of sunlit open square in front
of him, he was unable to get closer.

Instead, as Lane watched, the plucky ostler did
the next best thing. In a jinking, darting run, he set
out across the square, taking a line parallel to the
bank that made him a difficult target to hit and took

him towards Lije Coombs's hearse that was slewed broadside on to the bank building but some thirty yards away from its open doors.

A rifle cracked, twice, in quick succession. Dust spurted in front of Blue Hills's pounding feet. He stumbled, kept running, snapped a wild shot towards the bank intended to rattle the man with the rifle. A third shot rang out, and his hat flew skywards. Then he had reached the hearse's broad shadow. With a high-pitched yell of triumph he hurled himself forwards, landed on his feet behind the big black coach and flattened himself with his back to the woodwork.

Then Lane shifted his gaze, saw Blade Quatro. He was in the alley between the bank and the café, crouched down against the bank's stone walls. He held a Winchester rammed into his shoulder. His moustachioed face was pressed to the stock. He fired again. The shot cracked out, the bullet screaming harmlessly off the hearse's iron-clad wheel.

Behind Quatro, three terrified horses were rolling their eyes and tossing their heads. Their taut, straining reins were looped around Quatro's left wrist.

'Arkle! Slaughter!' Quatro roared. 'Get a move on, I can't hold 'em much longer.'

The tall, rangy figure of Zac Slaughter appeared in the bank's doorway. His six-guns were in their greased holsters. As he appeared in the opening, Blade Quatro tossed him the Winchester. Slaughter caught it deftly, snapped it to his shoulder and blasted two shots towards the hearse. Shards of shiny black wood flew high, and as a howl of rage rang out Lane saw Lije Coombs ahead of Blue Hills, an angular black shape pressed up against his beloved hearse's woodwork, doing his best to calm the frantic chestnut tangled in the traces.

Close enough now to do damage, Blue Hills ducked down, squinted under the hearse and fired three fast shots towards the bank. The slugs peeled strips of wood off the door panels close to Slaughter and whined into the bank. Slaughter snapped his head back and slid out of sight. But the sunlight still glinted on his rifle barrel, and Lane knew he was watching, and dangerous.

And Blade Quatro had already stepped around one of the plunging horses and taken a second Winchester from a scabbard.

It was clear to Rockwell Lane that this was a classic stand off that would end in the bandits making their escape, unless he thought of something fast. Mick Reilly was courageous, but in the wrong place. Blue Hills had cleverly worked his way closer to the bank, but against accurate fire from two rifles he could advance no further. The rest of the town had opted out. On the other side of the square the gunsmith had enough weapons and ammunition to equip an army but was staying put behind bolted doors. The store was boarded up after Dave Wilson's death. The Widow Logan had closed and locked the door of the rooming house – probably under instructions from a masterful Lije Coombs.

There would be no help forthcoming.

'Mick!'

The big saloon keeper glanced towards the stable, flashed a cheery grin.

'Mick, keep their heads down with that scatter gun, I'm coming across.'

Reilly lifted a hand. As Lane took a deep breath and sprinted out into the open, the saloonkeeper swung down on the bank, aimed high and fired one barrel of the shotgun, then glanced across to gauge Lane's progress.

A crack appeared in the bank's big window. Buckshot pattered off glass and brickwork. A horse squealed in fright and backed away on stiff legs. Blade Quatro's curses rang out as he struggled to hold onto the reins and pick off Reilly with the Winchester. The horse jerked again as he managed a fast shot. The slug winged high, shattering the window over the Pleasure Palace's gallery.

Lane was running fast, arms pumping, already halfway across the square. He ran in a straight line, keeping the big hearse between him and the jayhawkers. Blue Hills turned, anxiously watched his approach. Then Mick Reilly let go the shotgun's second barrel, and as Blade Quatro returned the fire from the alley and the square echoed to the thunder of the shotgun and the lighter crack of the Winchester, Rockwell Lane reached the hearse and took cover against the smooth black coachwork alongside one big rear wheel.

'Lije,' he panted. 'Sneak round, cut loose your horse. I want this coach manoeuvred over to the bank.'

'What's left of it,' Coombs lamented, and Lane could have sworn there were tears in the lofty man's eyes.

'It's all we've got – with luck maybe all we'll need,' Lane said. He gave the tall man a push, watched him delve into one capacious pocket of his frock-coat and come up with a folding knife, then said to Hills, 'What the hell happened, Blue?'

'All three of 'em came out the alley,' Hills said, crouching low, eyes fixed on the two bandits outside the bank. 'I'd worked things out with Moffatt, but they must've been holed up in the Mission San Luis, came in the wrong side of town.' He glanced at Lane's empty holster, said, 'I guess they gave you the slip, after some trouble. Where's Rivers?'

'Out at the Running Irons with a bullet hole in his back.'

'Not the best place for 'im to be,' Hills said. 'If I read Moffatt aright, Sam Wallace could turn out to be the purest poison.'

The big hearse jolted. It was followed by Lije Coombs's satisfied exclamation as the traces parted. Then a shrill squeal followed by a flash of glistening hide and the rapidly receding tattoo of hooves told of the chestnut horse's joy at being free.

'Swing her around, Blue,' Lane said.

He climbed to his feet, clamped his gloved hands on top of the big rear wheel, applied pressure and began to rotate it forwards. Hills leaped in front of him and, grunting with effort, began hauling on the spokes. With Coombs's stringy muscles heaving in similar fashion on the front wheel on that same side, the coach began to swing until it was facing the bank.

Blade Quatro caught on fast. He yelled a warning to Zac Slaughter, then, ignoring the plunging horses, he crossed to the opposite side of the alley so that he could see along the hearse that was now trundling slowly towards the bank.

He fired four shots, working the Winchester's glittering lever hard and fast. The range was now almost point blank. Lije Coombs was closest to the gunman. He jerked, grunted, and went down on one knee. The coach began to slew. Then Quatro's hammer clicked, and he dropped back, cursing, to reload.

'Other side,' Lane panted, salt sweat dripping from his chin. Blue Hills left him, leaped across the back of the hearse and applied his weight to the offside wheel. The coach straightened, and again moved forward relentlessly.

'Lije?' Lane called.

'Got me in the leg, ain't bad,' the tall man moaned. He had been left stranded as the hearse rolled away, and was lying crumpled and bleeding in the hot dust of the square.

Another volley of shots rang out as Zac Slaughter joined in Quatro's attempts to stop Blue Hills and the Texas Ranger. Chips of white wood flew from the hearse's coachwork. Bullets spanged off the iron-rimmed wheels. But now Lane and Hills had left the wheels and were able to shelter behind the hearse as they braced their legs and used their shoulders against the woodwork.

'We get close,' Rockwell Lane gritted, 'at my word we give this thing a final heave then go one down either side and give those jayhawkers a taste of lead—'

'Slaughter! Quatro!'

This was a new voice, a voice yelling from inside the bank with power and authority.

Jake Arkle, Lane guessed. And even as the thought entered his mind that for the first time he was close to the man he and Rivers had been ordered to apprehend, he heard the slamming of the bank's doors and the rattle of iron bolts.

'Hell, now what?'

He poked his head around the side of the hearse in time to see Blade Quatro leap back from the entrance to the alley. The outlaw loosened the looped reins from his wrist just enough to give him space to move, fumbled for a swinging stirrup, threw his stiff left leg over the back of a lean buckskin and clawed his way into the saddle. Then he was whooping and hollering, driving the horses hard down the alley and away from the square.

'Going out the bank's back door!' Blue Hills shouted. He hammered his fist in fury against the back of the rolling hearse, then drew his six-gun and ran for the alley.

'Wait!' Rockwell Lane yelled. He reached out clawed fingers for the ostler's shoulder as he went past. His hand slipped away as Hills lifted an arm and shrugged him off. Knowing what was going to happen, Lane ran wide, dropped to one knee, lifted the Winchester.

Blue Hills reached the mouth of the alley. As he did so the three outlaws appeared at the other end, mounted now, their horses snorting and wheeling and pawing the air in a yellow cloud of dust. A pair of heavy sacks was slung behind Jake Arkle's pommel. Six-guns flashed in the brilliant sunlight.

Blue Hills dropped into a crouch, began triggering his .45. Lane aimed for Jake Arkle, blasted a shot, saw the shot wing high and as Arkle spurred out of danger he shifted his aim and again squeezed the trigger. Blade Quatro roared in agony. His six-gun flew from his hand, spinning high and glittering in the air. Then Zac Slaughter was blazing away with each of his six-guns in turn, throwing down a hail of lead that sent stone chips flying, plucked like hot claws at Blue Hills's shirt, drove him back with stinging eyes and a sense that all about him was madness, sent him tumbling flat on his back.

Coolly, Rockwell Lane continued to fire into the whirling chaos of horses, men and billowing dust clouds. But now the outlaws had turned to make their escape. Raking spurs glittered. Hooves flashed. In an instant the raiders had spurred their mounts past the line of the building and beyond his sight. With his last shot Lane thought he saw Slaughter jerk backwards, arching, one hand clawing for the sky.

Then they were gone. The drum of their hooves was like the excited pumping of blood in his ears.

Lane was conscious of a constricting tightness in his throat. He swallowed, saw Blue Hills climbing dazedly to his feet; turned, saw Lije Coombs limping forlornly to the hearse and running his bony hands over the glistening white scars.

'Your leg?' Lane said with vague concern. The undertaker grimaced, turned away from the badly scarred coach and said, 'I'm so darn skinny the bullet couldn't find nothing vital, scratched me and flew off in disgust.'

Mick Reilly, red faced and indignant, came pounding across from his Pleasure Palace. There was the harsh sound of bolts being drawn. The bank's doors were flung open and Alan Moffatt came storming down the steps. Blue Hills had recovered his hat, came over towards the hearse poking a finger through the bullet hole, then planted it on his head.

'They took every damn cent!' Moffatt shouted. His face was damp and chalk white, his prominent eyes darting wildly.

'We'll get it back,' Lane said. 'We know where they are, where they're headed.'

'That's as maybe – but where the hell where you when it mattered?' Moffatt demanded loudly, insolently. 'Out chasing shadows, I suppose, when I had already tried to elicit from you your official capacity and you had—'

'What you tried to do was protect Sam Wallace and convince me outlaws like Jake Arkle can change their ways,' Lane drawled. 'Now you'd best keep your damn mouth shut, go back inside the bank, or maybe convene a meeting of Concho Flats town councillors and try to figure out where the hell you went wrong. Me, I've got some outlaws to catch.'

He turned his back on the stunned, speechless banker, and said to the grinning undertaker, 'Lije, things have taken a turn that Blue thinks will have put Charlie Rivers in some danger. I want you to catch that fine horse, hook this hearse up, go on out to the Running Irons and bring Charlie into town. Think you can handle that?'

'With me along, he can,' Mick Reilly offered. 'Blackie Nelson'll be happy to sit on the gallery, drink a cool beer and gaze across at that stable he hankers after.' He hefted the shotgun, winked at Blue Hills, and as the lanky undertaker limped off in search of the runaway chestnut the saloonkeeper tossed the scatter gun onto the hearse's high seat and began untangling the slashed traces.

Lane jerked his head at the ostler, and as the bank's doors slammed behind Alan Moffatt they fell in together and ran the hundred yards across the square to the livery stables. They reached the shadows cast by the high building, slowed, and breathing hard walked into the cool of the runway.

'Blue, you say those bank robbers rode in from the Mission San Luis?' Lane said, panting. 'You know any reason they'd do that?'

Hands on hips, chest heaving, Blue Hills said, 'They'll be heading for the border. If they've got sense they'll have spare horses. Leavin' them at the

Mission puts them a short step in the right direction.

'Damn!' Lane swore softly. 'I don't doubt you'll sell me a spare mount, Blue, but that puts me and those bandits no better than equal and means a long ride ahead.'

'Maybe,' Hills said. The ostler indicated Lane's waiting dun, and said, 'Ain't nothing wrong with the gelding a good rest won't cure – but with a real fast horse you could catch those jayhawkers within ten, fifteen miles, finish this today.'

A faint, knowing smile twitched at Rockwell Lane's lips.

'Yeah, I heard about those classy blue grass animals,' he said. 'Sure would appreciate the loan of one of those – but I guess there's a hefty price.'

'Double-barrelled, at that,' Blue Hills warned, his blue eyes carefully averted. 'I ride with you today, if I shape up okay I get to wear one of them stars in a silver circle permanent, Blackie Nelson gets himself a stable. But, hell, what I'm asking likely ain't in your power to give. . . .' He shrugged carelessly, stepped in through the open door of the office, slid open a drawer and took out a Colt .45 which he tossed to Lane.

'I've got one ranger laid up bad wounded,' Rockwell Lane said as he caught the six-gun and slid it into his holster, 'three felons on the run with cash they've stolen by violent means from a bank – and one of 'em's an outlaw wanted in every state or territory from Virginia clear to the Mex border.' He grinned. 'I guess you've just become a Texas Ranger by pure accident, Blue – so you'd best prepare those two fine horses for a fast and furious ride, and get yourself ready for your first official gunfight.'

THIRTEEN

Although the shortest distance to the Mexican border at Ciudad Acuña was naturally a straight line, taking that route across the terrain south of Concho Flats was difficult for a man unless he sprouted eagle's wings.

Texas Ranger Blue Hills figured correctly that the three jayhawkers weren't that smart. He also told Rockwell Lane that, unless they were sure of the way, after some fifteen miles the raiders would likely find their flight slowed considerably by a system of rocky arroyos that led into a wider draw which drained winter floodwaters into the Pecos.

'I reckon at this rate all five of us'll arrive there about the same time,' Lane said, with awe in his voice. 'I ain't never had anything this fast between my legs.'

He knew Charlie Rivers would have a quick retort, and smiled faintly at the thought. But truth was he had been so impressed by the sleek bay that Hills led out of the stall he had felt ashamed to be tainting its glossy coat with his travel-stained old McClellan.

That shame had been banished by the sheer exhilaration of the ride once he was in the saddle. As the hearse rattled out of the square with Coombs and Reilly sharing the seat, the two rangers rode out of town in a hurry and swept past the crumbling walls of the deserted Mission San Luis at a wondrous, stretched-out gallop. Five miles further on the two thoroughbreds had barely raised a sweat. Another five miles, and in an arid area dotted with pecans and live-oak thickets, the dust of the outlaws' recent passing was a thin haze still hanging in the hot air.

They were being rapidly overhauled.

'Arroyos comin' up,' Blue Hills called into the wind.

Rockwell Lane squinted ahead, saw the undulating grassland breaking up and the sun-baked horizon becoming serrated as the arroyos cut into the land, and at their edges rock slabs stood proud where centuries of rain had washed away the soil.

Then, abruptly, shockingly, a shot rang out, its flat echoes slapping across the rutted landscape to peter out into an aching silence. But already the surprised rangers were hurling themselves from the saddle, the two thoroughbreds high-stepping away as their riders desperately hugged the dry earth and wriggled on their bellies into deep grass tufting from beneath heavy boulders, sweeping off Stetsons to poke their heads around the rocks in an effort to locate the drygulcher.

A second shot cracked in the dry stillness. The

slug smacked into the granite boulders, chipping glistening splinters that keened off into the sun.

'Couple of hundred yards due south,' Lane said happily, rolling back behind the rock and dashing the salt sweat from his brow. 'Top of an easy slope beyond that stand of trees, tucked in behind a ridge of jagged rocks.'

'Kinda careless,' Hills said, surprise in his voice as he looked where Lane indicated. 'The top of a hat's showin', sun's catchin' a rifle barrel.'

'But we're still pinned down, saddle guns way off with the horses.'

'Nope, we go after him, there's more'n enough cover to get close with six-guns,' Hills said, parting thick grass with his gloved hands for a clearer view. 'He caught us cold, but that was his one chance and he blew it.'

'Maybe, maybe not,' Lane said with reservation. 'Somewhere out there there's a couple more tough hombres. And as for cover, you've read it right up to the last fifty or so yards – then it's a suicidal charge across open ground.'

Blue Hills's eyes crinkled as he grinned. 'All them years of experience 've made you over-cautious, Ranger. The way I read it they left one man behind to pick us off, catch up later. Open ground or not, that makes favourable odds.'

'Well, I thought I winged Zac Slaughter,' Lane mused. 'Could be you're right, pard, and I know Charlie Rivers'sd agree with your reasoning.' He drew the borrowed six-gun, swiftly checked the

loads, ran a hand along his gunbelt's filled loops.
'We'll outflank him. He'll know what we're doing,
but he can't shoot two ways at the same time. Stay
thirty, forty yards off to the side. When I whistle,
move in fast.'

Lane slapped Blue Hills's shoulder, watched the
former ostler roll clear of the boulder and take off
at a crouching run for a thick clump of mesquite.
Then he sucked in a deep lungful of air, burst from
behind the boulder on the opposite side and
sprinted thirty yards, clamping his teeth against the
pain of a barked knee as he dropped awkwardly to
lie flat at the bottom of a shallow depression.

The sun blazed down on a sweltering silence.
Mesquite branches trembled. The two horses
grazed. Rockwell Lane's heart thudded in his chest.

He blinked sweat from his eyes, risked lifting his
head. From his new position the gunman was out of
sight away to the left. But Lane could now see past
the first line of jagged rocks at the crest of the slope.
Beyond, higher still, where a flat slab of smooth
rock jutted from the side of the slope, a big bay
horse was ground-tethered.

With a bullet graze on its flank, Lane surmised,
and grunted with satisfaction. One man – but they
were by no means out of the woods.

The horse was Zac Slaughter's. Lane recalled the
numb horror of watching Slaughter spur that horse
alongside a pretty girl lying face down with her long
hair floating on the waters of the Concho, pump
bullets into her slender back and raise his fist in

triumph as his wild eyes glinted and he roared with laughter.

Zac Slaughter was born mean. Holed up in rocks under the searing midday sun, packing a bullet in his hide, he would be as dangerous as a cornered she-bear with cubs.

Gritting his teeth, Lane pulled in another deep, hissing breath and came up out of the depression in a rush. He covered the remaining 150 yards in a lung-searing, darting run, ducking and weaving, skin prickling, muscles tensed for the bullet that would shatter his heart without his ever hearing the whisper of its coming.

His mad dash took him up onto a wide, sloping ridge between two arroyos, no more than thirty yards to the right of Zac Slaughter's position that was now hidden from him by straggling growths of parched mesquite.

As he dropped flat behind a stunted live-oak, chest heaving, sweat stinging his eyes, Lane saw the flutter of a faded blue shirt against green chaparral as Blue Hills went to ground the same distance on the other side of the outlaw.

If he could see the ostler from where he was, Lane reasoned, at half the distance, so could Slaughter. But still there was no reaction. Why?

Because, Lane decided bitterly, despite what old Blue said, the man knows all he's got to do is sit there with his rifle and pick us off as we run at him like two naked chickens over those last few yards of open ground.

But it had to be done – and fast!

Rockwell Lane dragged a hand down across his wet face, wiped both sticky palms on his pants, drew his .45. Then, fixing himself into a low crouch with a steadying hand on the ground and one leg braced behind him, he let loose with a piercing whistle – and with a fierce, powerful lunge drove himself forwards.

He burst clear of the live-oak, leaped over the straggling mesquite, felt his spurs snag then broke clear and let loose with a wild rebel yell. In the distance, the slight figure of Blue Hills was already flapping up from the ground like a startled rooster and suddenly the beginning of uncontrollable mirth was bubbling up in Lane's throat, his eyes blurring with tears.

Like the thin echo of his own scream, Blue Hills's banshee wail split the hot, heavy silence. Then, as Rockwell Lane choked back hysterical laughter, the two rangers were converging at speed, bounding across the hard ground, hurdling rocks and bushes, pistols held high and flashing in the sunlight, charging down on the jagged rocks behind which a man waited with a rifle to kill them.

A dead man.

'Judas Priest!' Lane panted, hauling to a standstill.

Blue Hills gasped, spat wetly in disgust.

Zac Slaughter was propped up with his back against the rocks. His hat was rammed down on his head. His blind eyes were rolled back and milk white. The butt of his Winchester was jammed in a crevice, the barrel positioned to reflect the sun.

'Well,' Rockwell Lane said hoarsely, 'someone sure as hell took a shot at us.'

'That was me,' Jake Arkle called from behind them, and as the hair on Lane's neck prickled and he spun fast, whipping up his six-gun, knowing it was far, far too late, a shot rang out and Blue Hills was driven backwards to fall with a choking gasp into the dead arms of Zac Slaughter.

Jake Arkle was thirty yards away against the high rocks, standing square and spread-legged, a smoking six-gun in his big right fist and a wolfish smile splitting his dark, whiskered countenance.

Blade Quatro was to his right. Their facets catching the high, hot sun, the round silver conchos ornamenting the raffish outlaw's black hat reflected flashes of dazzling light. His teeth were glistening white under his flowing moustache. Still unsteady on his injured left leg, he supported himself with one hand braced against the smooth rock slab. In the other hand his remaining six-gun was held high and cocked. He stood as taut as a coiled spring, cruel black eyes ever watchful, leaving the killing to Arkle but tensed to spring into violent action if called on and cut down the rangers with a hail of hot lead.

All of this Lane took in with one sweeping glance as he finished his lightning-fast turn and flung himself sideways. His shoulder hit the ground with a bone-jarring thud. He rolled, spinning like a stiff log on the slope. A six-gun cracked, and his hat flew off. Another bullet drilled closer. Dirt kicked up into his face. He spat, came out of the roll, spun on his hands and toes and sprang sideways into a crouch as a bullet hissed through his hair.

Arkle was growling his fury, desperately swinging his six-gun to follow the ranger's bewildering movements. Abruptly Lane stopped, lifted his six-gun. His first shot took Arkle in the chest. Out of the corner of his eye he saw Quatro move, and dropped to one knee as Jake Arkle slammed back against the rock, eyes shocked wide, mouth slack.

Quatro's mouth twisted into a snarl. He stepped away from the rock. His .45 came up. He whipped his left arm across his body, fanned the hammer with the edge of his hand. Three rapid shots cracked out, the bullets singing.

Brushed by death, Lane hurled himself to the ground. He landed on his left hand and forearm, felt pain knife through his hip. Quatro's six-gun swung, the muzzle black and gaping. Lane flipped up his hand, snapped a shot at the outlaw. The bullet punched into the centre of his fancy silk vest. Quatro quivered, stumbled backwards, hands dropping. Lane saw the dark hole appear, the sudden flare of bright red blood. Jaw muscles knotted, he steadied his aim and shot Blade Quatro cleanly in the centre of his sweat-streaked forehead.

Time was standing still.

Quatro died slowly, the six-gun drooping then clattering to the ground as dead fingers uncurled.

Jake Arkle was still standing, but his eyes were gazing into eternity and his legs were crumpling.

Rockwell Lane pouched his six-gun and leaped to the dying man's side, caught him in the circle of his arm and eased him down the smooth rock into a helpless sprawl in which there was no strength.

'You got the cash,' Arkle gasped, 'but it's too late for Wallace.' His jaw hung loose. Blood welled from his mouth, dribbled onto his woollen shirt.

'You're not making sense,' Lane said.

'Sure.' Jake Arkle attempted a grin, choked, sucked in a bubbling breath as Lane waited. 'Hercules Irons,' Arkle whispered then, 'not Sam Wallace. High up official, walked out of a bank in Virginny with enough cash to set himself up and ruin my family. Took me all this . . . all these years . . . got word from the kid, Vern, out to pay back his old man. . . .'

He stopped, wheezing, his eyes glazing. Lane stripped off his bandanna, dabbed the blood from the outlaw's mouth. Arkle shook his head, flapped feebly with a hand. 'Irons could've took the loss of his herd. But once I stole his cash . . . he was finished here. Even if he gets it back, the story comes out . . . over . . . finished here . . . move on fast. . . .'

'The Running Irons,' Lane said, and cursed himself for a fool. 'Saw his picture in a newspaper in Austin. That and the ranch name should have told me who he was.' He shook his head. 'You should have stayed clear, Jake, rode west like you told that gal in Santa—'

'He's dead, Rocky.'

Lane looked up to see Blue Hills, white faced, hugging a blood soaked arm, and he took a deep breath.

'I guess if you heard all that you'll know I'm a blind fool – and if Irons has rode on like Arkle says, we've still got work to do.'

He lowered Jake Arkle to the hard ground, said, 'Come on, Blue, let's get these fellers loaded up and take Moffatt's cash back to town.'

It took them some time.

They rode back into Concho Flats when the sun was red at their backs, and as they crossed the rutted square the hearse squealed in on the other side of town with a dry axle and Mick Reilly bulky on the seat.

Lije Coombs was atop Charlie Rivers's blue roan, black frock coat flaring gracefully, and as they watched he jolted proudly across the square to where the Widow Logan waited outside the rooming house – and promptly fell off at her feet.

'Charlie's in the back,' Reilly said when they reached him, his sharp blue eyes taking in the grisly burdens roped on the trail horses, the two rangers atop the glistening thoroughbreds. 'When Lije climbs up out've the dust he'll arrange for him to stay with the widow till he's healed, got his strength back. Looks like Charlie'll get to test the widow's cold bed before Lije.' He indicated the bulging sacks. 'Moffatt's gone home, but I see you got Arkle, and the cash.'

Lane nodded. 'You see Sam Wallace at the ranch?'

'Yep. Seems when the Running Irons and Vern Wallace pulled out they took the whole damn remuda with them. Only way Wallace could leave was on Charlie's horse – and Charlie objected.'

'Jesus!' Lane breathed. 'Charlie in that condition – and he bested Sam Wallace?'

Reilly nodded. 'Forgot to tell you. Wallace is also in the back of the hearse.' He grinned. 'Put him on the floor, gave Charlie pride of place – he's all tucked up inside that shiny coffin.'

'The way I feel,' Blue Hills said in a voice tight with pain, 'I'd swap places with him right now.'

Reilly cocked a speculative eye at the little ostler and said, 'Looks like you got off to a bad start in a good job, Blue. You best get yourself inside the Pleasure Palace, take a couple of pulls of strong liquor before Blackie Nelson comes across from his new stable with his blacksmith tools, starts digging for that slug – but first I'll get Charlie fixed up.'

He clicked his tongue and the weary chestnut lifted its drooping head and moved the battered hearse off across the square. The movement must have woken the injured Charlie Rivers. First an arm appeared over the white satin lining, waving feebly, then a tousled head, and before they'd rattled and squealed fifty yards a befuddled Texas Ranger was sitting bolt upright in the coffin and gazing out groggily through the shattered ornamental glass.

'And if I didn't know exactly what was going on,' Rockwell Lane said, sliding down from the sleek horse and flipping the reins over the hitch rail outside the Pleasure Palace, 'I'd be feelin' a darn sight worse than Charlie Rivers – and right now he can't make out if he's landed in heaven, or the other place!

'Come on, Blue, let's go get that drink.'